AF480659

A SUMMER *Romance*

JESSE APLAND

ISBN: 979-8-89031-441-3 (sc)
ISBN: 979-8-89031-442-0 (hc)
ISBN: 979-8-89031-443-7 (e)

Because of the dynamic nature of the Internet, any web addresses or links contained in this book may have changed since publication and may no longer be valid. The views expressed in this work are solely those of the author and do not necessarily reflect the views of the publisher, and the publisher hereby disclaims any responsibility for them.

One Galleria Blvd., Suite 1900, Metairie, LA 70001
(504) 702-6708
1-888-421-2397

Chapter 1

$\mathcal{K}$endra pole vaults in the air and knocks the bar off the stand. She lands on the mat with the bar and I go flying in the air with my phone in my hand. It's May and today is the last day of track practice. This weekend is State Track. I'm sitting on the mat while I wait for my best friend to get done practicing her pole vaulting. I'm the manager of the small track team. Everyone else has left and gone home. The only ones left are me, my friend, Kendra, and her young coach Ben. I'm sitting on the mat, relaxing in my t-shirt and jeans, enjoying the warmth of the sun. My hair is blowing in the gentle breeze. I'm playing with my Tracfone while Kendra does her last jump. She pole vaults in the air, and Ben yells, "K! Now turn and push." Just as Kendra goes over the bar, she turns and pushes the pole away. She lands on the mat and I go flying in the air again.

Kendra has always been a good jumper. The only thing I was good at was long-distance running. That ended, though, in last August when I dislocated my kneecap. Right before cross-country season of my senior year. Yeah. I was pretty bummed. I was in therapy the entire season. If I dislocate it again, I will have to go in for surgery. So now my mom forbids me to run ever again. That is why I'm a manager in my last year of track. Poo.

"You will do good this weekend," Ben says as he pats Kendra's back.

I'm finishing up cleaning out my contact list on my Tracfone. It's time to gather the equipment and put the pole vaulting stuff away for the year. It's a little bittersweet – another season in the books and in a couple of days we will be high school graduates. I'm about to stand up and put my phone in my pocket when Ben walks up to me.

"Hey, Jess. I was wondering if I could have your phone number now that I see you have a phone." I'm shocked. I mean - I have known Ben since my freshman year, and we share at least one thing in common: we both like cats. He is good-looking, too, with his short blonde hair and ocean blue eyes. All the girls in high school knew that too. Why would he want my number? I look at Kendra, and her mouth is wide open. I guess she's shocked too that he asked for my number. Especially since I also knew that Kendra liked him.

"No, I can't," I said.

Ben looked down. I think I hurt his feelings. I *had* to say no. Kendra is my best friend. I couldn't take the man that my best friend has a crush on. I did that once to one of my other friends. She hated me for it. I didn't want to do that to Kendra.

We start cleaning up in silence. Kendra tidies up her clothes and pole. Ben and I start taking the stand apart and putting it away. I whisper to Ben, "I can give you my phone number, but I have to do it when Kendra isn't around. Meet me in the parking lot in a couple of minutes."

Ben nods his head then runs across the football field and into the school to get to the parking lot. I pick up Kendra's pole since her hands are full with her spikes and warm-up clothes. I help her get everything into the gym. I put her pole in the storage room where it can easily be seen tomorrow morning to be picked up for the track meet. She goes inside the locker room to change her clothes.

"See you in the morning, Kendra!"

"Bye!" she yells back.

I walk back out of the gymnasium, onto the foyer, and into the parking lot. I see Ben leaning against his blue car. Wow! He looks hot with the sun beating down on him. I stick my hands in my pockets and start making my way toward him. He gets his phone out as if anxiously waiting for my number.

"I'm only giving you my number because I didn't want to hurt your feelings," I said. "Kendra likes you, so I didn't want to give you my number in front of her. It would hurt her feelings." Ben seemed to understand, but didn't say anything. I gave him my digits and said good-bye.

On my drive home, which is a 15-mile drive outside of town, I kept thinking to myself: *Did I handle that right? I hope Kendra doesn't find out. If Kendra does find out, what will happen? I hope she won't hate me. Been there, done that.* Then I shifted my thoughts to Ben and how great he looked today. Too bad I won't get to see him this weekend. He must have to work or something since he is missing the state track meet. I didn't know when I was going to see him again. Maybe that's why he wanted my number. Maybe he wanted to know how everyone is doing at the track meet, especially Kendra since he is the pole vaulting coach. Yeah, that's what I'm going with. It makes me feel less guilty about my feelings.

Chapter 2

Saturday is the last day of state track. By the end of the day, the only event the team won is the Girls 4 x 800-meter relay; they placed third. I haven't heard from Ben since that moment in the parking lot. The entire time I've been here, I've been checking my phone, hoping for a call or a text asking if Kendra did well. Nothing.

The sun is warm, but the air is cool. I'm sitting on the grass soaking up the rays, kind of disappointed. I hear chatter and blow guns going off to start races. I look up from the grass to watch Kendra do her last pole vault, and she nails it! Seven feet and, six inches high. She didn't do as well as she did earlier, which was 8 feet, but she placed 8th! Whoo hoo! Go, Kendra! Overall, the team got 16th out of 19. Not the best the team has done, so the two hour ride home was pretty quiet. When we are out in the middle of nowhere, my Tracfone dings. As I'm digging the phone out of my pocket, I'm thinking, "It's probably my mom wondering when I'm coming home." I flip open my phone, and I see an unknown number with a message. The message reads How did you guys do this weekend? Oh, how excited I am to see that text message! I told him about the girl's relay race and how Kendra got 8th. Ben: Sounds like u guys did awesome!

Ben: What time is your graduation tomorrow?

Me: 2 o'clock. R u coming?

Ben: I am. I'm coming to watch u and Kendra walk on stage.

Me: That's sweet! Glad u r coming.

Ben: ☺

I closed my phone and slipped it in my pocket. I couldn't help but smile the rest of the ride home.

When we get back to the school, Kendra asks, "Why are you so happy? You were smiling all the way home." I couldn't help but blush.

"I met a guy today," I lied, trying not to tell her about Ben.

"Ooooh. Do tell," she pushes. I hate that. She is going to make me blurt it out.

"Well, he is cute and of course has blue eyes." I didn't lie about that.

"Are you going to see him again?" she asks.

"I don't know, but I did get his phone number." I didn't lie about that either.

"Cool! You have to tell me how you met," she pushes on.

"I can't," I said. "Maybe some other time. I'll see you tomorrow." I leave before she asks me anymore questions. I'm glad she cares and is interested, but I didn't want to tell her about Ben. At least not yet.

Sunday is Graduation day. I'm so nervous. I don't know why, but I am. I think it's because this is it. The last day of being a kid. Once I cross that stage, I am in uncharted territory. I will be considered an adult, expected to go out into the world, to find my place in life. Yikes! It is scary.

We skip church this morning because of the big day. There is so much to do before the graduation ceremony even begins, and family is starting to show up. I'm dressed up in my layered, white skirt with a dressy, peach t-shirt under my cap and gown, which is white with gold trimming. For some unknown reason, that is what my classmates chose for our gowns when our school colors are black and gold. For my shoes, I decide to wear my high heeled light-up shoes. I wore them for prom first, but I can't help it. I love these shoes! They light up when I step down. Kind of like those tennis shoes when I was little. They light up when I stepped down.

Anyways, my uncle owns this 1992 red corvette, and he drove it to my house. I begged for a ride, so he drove me to my graduation in his shiny, classy car. *Shriek!* I. Am. So Cool! Of course, no one got to see me in it because we had to park so far away from the school. The crowds were incredibly thick. I had to walk a block in my light up high heeled shoes. My feet already hurt.

Graduation starts with us walking down the aisle with "Pomp and Circumstance." Of course. Tradition. We sit down in our designated chairs. We got this, after having practiced it for 2 hours on Thursday morning at school with the entire senior class. Once everyone is settled, a few people start with their speeches, including our valedictorian. Then it's time for the choir to sing. I'm the only senior in Choir; I have to get up and walk across the gym to the stand. I find this extremely embarrassing! It's like crickets in the background and my shoes are making the click, clack sounds on the hardwood floor. It seems like it takes me forever to get there and when I do, I take my spot in the middle space on the stand that is saved for me. I still stick out like a sore thumb because I'm the only one in cap and gown, and…yeah… it had to be white!

A guy calls out from my class, "Sing out loud, Jess!" Oh geez.

While we are singing, my eyes are scanning the crowd for Ben. I can't find him, and I feel a slight twinge of disappointment. He either blends in well, or else he didn't show. After we sing one song, we all leave the choir stand and head to our seats. I practically sprinted to mine. Then it was time for our slideshow. Yay. Slides of baby pictures of us next to our senior pics. No one is going to guess me in my baby pictures because I look like a boy, especially when I'm in my uncle's football helmet and shoulder pads. Thank goodness there is only 28 of us graduating this year. (It's a really small school.)

The slide show went pretty fast. Finally…, diploma time. I get called first because my last name starts with a B, Brown. "Jessica A. Brown." I get up to walk up the stairs to the stage. I am beyond nervous. I know there is really nothing to it: grab my diploma, shake hands, pause for picture, and get off. I did just that. I didn't fall on my face or anything. I made it! I did it! I am a high school graduate and I am now considered an adult.

After everyone gets called and walks on stage, pomp and circumstance plays again and we leave the gym two by two. We line up in the hallway, letting people say their congratulations. I hug and shake hands with everyone who I practically know. Finally, I see Ben walking in line. He is getting closer. Do I hug him? Should I just shake his hand? What do I do? He's in front of me now. He hugs me.

"Congrats," he says.

I squeeze him back and say, "Thanks." He smells so good. Our hug ends.

Then I hear my cousin through the crowd. "We're going to your after party. We will see you there, okay?"

I wave and yell, "Okay!"

Ben asks, "You having an after-party? Where?"

"Well, I'm sharing an after party with a couple of others at the town hall. You can come if you want."

"Sure. I'll make my appearance." I can't help but smile after that comment.

After the long line ends, I'm finally able to go to the town hall and celebrate with my two other friends. There were a lot of people already there, and most of them signed my guest book. Even my old crush came up from college to our after-party. I didn't get a chance to talk to him because another old friend came to surprise me. It was an amazing surprise because I haven't seen her since elementary school. I did see Ben come by and talk to my classmates, but I don't know if he just didn't get a chance to talk to me, or if he felt like he already congratulated me back at school. Either way, it was fine because I was so busy talking to everyone there. I must admit, though, I couldn't help but keep an eye on him.

Chapter 3

*I*t's been a couple of weeks since graduation, and I started a new job and a new life. My dad got me a position where he works doing all sorts of paperwork. Even though we work at the same place, I still don't see him much because he has different hours and works in a different building. I show up for my hire orientation first thing in the morning. My goodness. There sure are a lot of guys working here. Of course, it's my hire orientation day, so I dress up somewhat nice. I have on teal khakis with a light pink undershirt and a see-through white tank top. My hair is up in a clip. I walk from the parking lot to the main entrance, and can feel the eyes of guys watching me as I slip into the building.

I'm a bit nervous. It's a new place with new people. I walk upstairs to the HR department and find out that I'm not the only one with orientation today. There are two other guys already waiting in the office. Their eyes are on me as I find a seat. I wish I had a book or a magazine to hide behind. Hire orientation surprisingly lasts all day. It includes rules and regulations, safety guidelines, and a tour. That was just in the morning. After our lunch break, we come back to meet our supervisor. My boss is quality control. She tells me what I will be doing this summer, which is entering data into the computer and cleaning out their attic. Cleaning their attic requires me to scan all the papers that are filed in all the boxes, then shred them. I am told there are like hundreds of boxes in the attic. My boss assures me I will not be able to get all of this done by the end of the summer, so I will have to return next summer. As I think about a guaranteed job for next summer, I am jolted into reality that college starts in three months, right before Labor Day weekend. I have about 100 days of work before adulthood really kicks in. Barely any time to have fun this summer. Poo.

I haven't heard from Ben in the last couple of weeks either. I am beginning to think that he only wanted my phone number to keep in contact for track. No biggie. I need to focus on my new life anyway. I have enough on my plate. I already have a caller anyway. His name is Colt. He's been calling me since I took a class trip to the Tetons in March. He doesn't call me every night, but close to it. We just talk. I don't think we are going to get past the friend stage anyway. Besides, I'm not attracted to him. There's got to be a spark. Otherwise, what kind of relationship would that be?

May ended, and it's now the beginning of June. The workplace is putting a fishing tournament on at the nearby lake, which is Keyhole Reservoir. My dad is coming back from a business trip this week. He told me we could enter the tournament together, especially since he loves to fish and hunt. I said, "Sure. Sounds like fun." If only Kendra were in town. I really want to bring a friend. Kendra went across the state for her job. I will see her again in college because we are sharing a dorm room. I thought it would be so much better sharing a room with her than a complete stranger. Maybe fishing with my dad won't be too bad. It will be a fun father/daughter time.

The weekend comes and it's time for the fishing tournament. I have to wake up earlier than usual to get to the reservoir and enter our names in on time. By the time we get there, the sun is completely up, and it's getting warm. I take off my baggy sweatshirt, which exposes my dark green striped tank top. I will change into shorts later when it gets too hot.

My dad unloads the boat into the greenish blue water. I'm already sitting in it because I have to drive it back to the dock while he parks the truck. Simple. I don't get to drive the boat often, but I got to this time. I watch my dad as he parks the truck up on the hill. He gets out and starts walking toward the dock. I slowly drive the boat back to where he is headed. My dad quickly hops in, and he takes over the steering wheel. I take my place on the other chair, and off we go!

My dad knows where to catch the wall-eye. We always go to the right places. We get to our first place, which is next to some cliffs. I look in the water to see if I can see the bottom. I can't, so I know it's deep. Dad puts the trolling motor in the water. I set up my pole, tie my jig head on, and put a minnow on the hook. It's fishing time. I throw my line in the lake away from the cliffs. Dad taught me well.

By the afternoon, I am eating sunflower seeds and I've changed into my shorts. I am relaxing with my line out in the water. It's so hot out now that I'm sweating just sitting here. I'm what you call trolling while my dad jigs on the other side of the boat. Jigging is casting then slowing reeling in, playing with the bait. He makes the boat move while he does this. Trolling is a matter of just sitting here, lazily waiting for the bite.

My Tracfone dings. I flip it open and it read What have u been doing? I smile knowing that Ben was thinking about me.

Me: I have been working.

Ben: Where r u working?

Me: M&K Contracting. My dad hooked me up since he works there.

Ben: That's cool. I have been working too.

Me: Where do u work?

Ben: At south mine.

Me: What r your hours like? My dad worked a lot when he worked at a mine.

Ben: My hours r long, but I get good money.

Me: That's good. ☺

Ben: So, what r u doing?

Me: I'm at Keyhole. Fishing with my dad.

Ben: I haven't been there in a while. R u catching anything?

Me: I caught one walleye so far. My dad has caught like 5, which is good because we are in a tournament.

Ben: A tournament!

Me: Yeah. It's just for work. We will be done at 4.

"Who are you texting?" my dad asks, breaking my concentration. "A guy," I said.

"Is it that guy that calls you like every night?" "No. It's a different guy." My phone dings again.

Ben: U need to keep catching some more fish then. Have fun!

Me: I will, but I didn't get to ask what r u doing? So….what r u doing?

"How many guys are calling you?" my dad asks. I guess he has a right to know what his daughter has been up to.

"Just the two now, I guess."

"What about that one guy you went out with earlier? I liked him."

I'm thinking, *but I didn't.*

"Are you still talking to him?"

"No, I'm not, Dad. I don't like him." All that guy wanted to do was get in my pants. He had more moves than an octopus. My phone dings again.

Ben: Cleaning house and doing laundry. Not much to do today.

Me: Life is pretty boring now that there is no track, huh?

Ben: Sort of. I just don't have a girl anymore to keep me busy when I'm not working.

I didn't know how to answer that. Was he trying to tell me something? I didn't want to take it the wrong way like maybe he was interested in me. Maybe he was just bored and wanted to talk to somebody.

"I know his dad," my dad continues. "I like his dad."

I'm thinking, *I don't care if you like his dad. I don't like him!*

My phone dings again. R u seeing anybody? I think that absence of a beat was my heart stopping. Is he interested in me?

Apparently, the excitement on my face showed because my dad asked, "Did he ask you out?" I immediately changed my expression.

"No. He just asked if I was seeing anybody."

"That's a good thing to ask," my dad offers. Then he asks, "Do I get to meet him?" "That depends if he takes me out on a date, and if he picks me up at the house." "Good point," my dad adds. I'm imagining Ben pulling into the driveway with his blue car. He gets out, and I see him in nice clothes. He walks up the stairs to where I'm standing on the deck. He holds out his hand for me to grab, and…. Oh, geez! I need to answer Ben. I quickly type: No, I'm not.

Chapter 4

During the next couple of weeks, Ben and I text back and forth on a regular basis. Nothing too serious. Just wondering what the other is doing and how everything's going. He is a sincere guy. I like that. He seems to care about how I'm feeling or what certain things I say mean. I feel like we are becoming good friends. The type of friends that could tell each other secrets, like me and Kendra. I was kind of doing that with Colt, but it seemed different with Ben. There is definitely a connection with Ben.

Finally! It's Friday, June 23rd. I am home from work and I'm cleaning out my lunchbox when the phone rings. It was Colt. He's calling a bit earlier than usual. We do our normal conversation, then I tell him I have to go so I can eat my dinner.

He says, "Wait. I wanna ask you something. Will you go out with me tomorrow night?" Now usually, I give every guy a chance to take me out at least once, but I've been talking a lot to Ben lately. It wouldn't be fair to him if I went out with some other guy when I told him I wasn't seeing anyone.

"I'm sorry, Colt. I didn't know you were interested in me, but I'm kind of seeing somebody else." There was silence on the other end.

"Sorry, Colt," I say again.

"It's okay," he finally says. "I got to go." Well, I crushed his spirit. He'll probably never call me again. But it might be for the best.

I go to my room and sit on my bed, feeling pretty bummed that I hurt somebody's feelings. My phone dings. I flip it open, and it says, How was your work week?

Me: It was good till now. I feel pretty bummed.

Ben: Y?

Me: The guy that has been calling me almost every day for the last 3 months now asked me out.

Ben: So y r u so bummed?

Me: I told him no and hurt his feelings. I hate doing that.

Ben: Y did u tell him no?

Me: Because u asked me earlier if I was seeing anybody. I wasn't. I thought he just wanted to be friends. Not anything more. Ben: He wanted something more?

Me: Yes.

Ben: I guess he should've told u a long time ago. He has been calling u for 3 months and he never told u how he felt?

Me: No he never did.

Ben: Sounds like a chicken to me. I wouldn't feel bad. If he wanted more, he should've asked u out a long time ago.

Ben was right. If Colt wanted more than just talking on the phone, he should've asked me out a long time ago. I was feeling better. Ben made me feel better.

Me: Thanks for putting that into perspective for me. I feel better. ☺

Ben: No prob.

In better spirits, I go out of my room and eat my dinner that my mom left on the table for me. It was getting cold. I finish eating, clean up the dishes, and put away the leftovers. I go back to my room to get ready to take a shower. I check my phone and notice that Ben wasn't done texting me. I quickly flip open the phone and read the message.

Ben: Since we r on the subject. I was wondering if we could go steady.

I feel bad for making him wait this long. I type:

Oh. Sorry. I had to eat dinner. It was getting cold. I would love to!

Ben: ☺

I go into the bathroom with a big smile on my face, and I sing at the top of my lungs in the shower! I step out of the shower, and slip into my jammies, and slide into bed. Laying there, I realized that we've got to go out on dates to go steady. Don't we? When are we going out on our first date? Thoughts like these keep swirling in my head until I finally fall asleep.

Since it was Saturday, I was able to sleep in. I wake up because my cat is doing her shiatzu massage on my back and purring, wanting me to get up and pet her. I love my Siamese kitty. Honestly, she is my one true friend in the whole entire world. Somehow, she knows when I'm upset because she snuggles up to me and let me cry into her fur when I have those moments. She knows my voice, too. When I call out, "Sbabys, my sweetness!" She comes running to me every time. I take care of her. I mean, besides feeding, watering, and cleaning out her litter box, I make sure she is safe when she is outside. I also keep her warm in the winter with blankets and a heating pad. She is getting old. I got her when I was seven, and now I'm eighteen, making her eleven years old. Each year, she seems more fragile.

As I turn over to pet her, I knock her over onto the bed, and I start petting her in that special way she loves. That really gets her motor going.

"Good morning to you too! So what are we going to do today?" Before I had a chance to pretend she could talk back to me, my phone dings. I reach over to my night stand and grab my phone, still petting Sbabys. I flip it open.

Ben: I want to see u again. I was up all night last night thinking when I could see u again. R u free for the 4th of July?

Me: Yes!

Ben: K. I think I got something planned. I will let u know more when the time gets closer.

Me: Sounds good!

I get out of bed, grab Sbabys, and make my way to the kitchen. My parents are sitting at the table, talking and drinking their coffee. My brother must still be sleeping.

"Well, I think that's the first time I've seen a smile from you first thing in the morning," my mom comments. Normally, I'm pretty cranky in the morning. I'm literally the person that can wear the shirt that says, "I don't do mornings." This morning, however, was different because Ben wants to see me again.

Chapter 5

All I could do at work, as I'm standing at the scanner, is think of Ben and how excited I am to see him again. This week seemed long. It was the last week of June, which meant 4th of July is right around the corner. Friday night, I get a text from him. It's a multi-media message, which means that he text his message to not just me, but to others as well.

I think I have a 4th of July party planned. We r going to Keyhole to have fun and celebrate. Bring your swimsuit, water, and your own lunch. Supper will be provided.

I text back asking if I need to bring anything to help with supper. He said no and that it was taken care of. By Sunday afternoon, I realize that I need to know what time to show up. I texted him to find out.

Ben: I was planning on leaving around 9-10 o'clock. Where do u live? I can pick u up. Me: I live 15 miles north of town. It is on the way for u. Just text me when u leave so I can be ready b4 u show up.

Finally! It's Tuesday, the 4th of July. I wake up the normal time that I would for work and get myself ready. I'm going to be wearing my swimsuit, so I make sure no hairs are visible. I carefully shave my legs and armpits, then wax my face. I also have my mom twist my hair then put it up into a ponytail. I automatically put on my swimsuit first, then my tank top and shorts over it. In my bag, I packed my undergarments and warm clothes. For lunch, I packed what I normally eat for work, which is a ham and cheese sandwich, chips, yogurt, and a Capri-sun. I slice up some carrots to eat as a snack, just in case I'm hungrier than usual. I also borrow one of my dad's one gallon water jugs. That should last me all day. I'm all packed and ready. I look at myself in the mirror. Do I need earrings? Naw. What about make-up? Maybe some water-proof mascara. That will do the trick. Sounds like I'm swimming anyway, and I don't want to be gussied up for that. I will, however, put my eye makeup in my bag just in case.

I sit in the recliner with my phone in my hand, expecting to hear from Ben at any minute. I'm watching the clock in front of me and rocking in my chair. 9:05. 9:15. He said 9 to 10. He may not leave until 10. I'm still rocking and watching the clock. 9:20. 9:30. My phone dings. There he is! OMW. (On My Way.) I continue rocking in the chair, keeping an eye on the clock.

It's about 9:45 now. He will be here any minute. I put my bag, lunch, and water next to the sliding glass door.

"Is he here?" my mom asks.

"Almost," I said.

My dad walks in the house. "I think he's here."

I look out the window, and I see the blue car driving up to the house. "Yep. That's him," I say. I pick up my bag, lunch, and water.

"Wait," my dad says. "Aren't you going to let him in the house?" I really didn't want to, but I guess my parents want to meet him. I mean, grill him. *Sigh*

Ben comes up to the door and knocks. I open the door with the stuff still in my hands.

"I'm ready," I said as I try to rush Ben back out to the car.

"Wait," Ben says. "Aren't your parents home?"

What?! He wants to meet my parents? That's new. Normally, the guys I go out on a date with don't even come to the front door. They honk me out to the car. I turn around to go back in the house with Ben behind me. My parents are standing in the kitchen waiting for an introduction.

"Mom, Dad, this is Ben. Ben, this is Bev and Fred." Ben shakes their hands.

My mom asks, "How late are you going to keep her?"

He answers, "Well, we will probably stay till the fireworks are over, so it may not be until midnight. Is that ok?"

Mom and Dad look at each other, look back at Ben, and then nod. Okay. Are my parents done grilling Ben?

"Can we go now?" I ask everyone.

Ben says, "Sure. Nice meeting you," as he waves to my parents.

I didn't wave to my parents. I just wanted Ben out of the house. I get myself down the deck steps and Ben catches up with me, grabbing my bag.

"Let me help you," he says.

He takes the bag off my shoulder and puts it into his trunk. Then he grabs my water jug and lunch bag and puts it into the trunk as well. I look back at the window and see Mom and Dad watching us. I wave to them. They wave back. I turn around and I see Ben getting into the car. I open the passenger door and slide in. The car was surprisingly clean, yet I could smell coal dust. Yep. He takes this car to work. In fact, this may be the only car he owns. That's okay. At least he's not like my dad, who owns like 13 trucks.

The drive out to Keyhole was quiet except for the classic rock station playing on the radio. When Ben takes the exit from the interstate to get to the reservoir, my excitement builds and I start wondering where exactly we are going. The place is going to be full of people because it's a holiday. The drive from the interstate to the lake is always beautiful with all the trees. Ben slows down and takes the first left. We are going to the marina? No. I bet we are going to the beach. Sure enough. Ben goes past the Marina and finds a parking spot next to the outhouses. Not the best parking, but the closest parking spots next to the beach are already taken. There sure are a lot of people here, which I kind of expected. By now it's close to 11 o'clock. I go around the car to the trunk to help Ben unload.

"Can I help you take anything to the beach?" I ask.

"Do you want to take your bag?" he asks.

"No, that can stay in the car. I just want my lunch box and water, but I can carry something else too."

Ben hands me a box. "Here. You can take this I guess."

I turn around and start heading my way to the beach. I wonder where he wants to settle on the sand. I get to the edge of the beach, put the box down, and turn around looking to see how far behind he is. He's coming. I'll wait for him here. The sun is already so hot that it's making the sand quite toasty. I swipe a drop of sweat from my forehead. I look out at the beach and see people laying on towels, talking, and eating. Kids are playing with balls and sand toys, running around, enjoying the freedom of the beach. I look at the water and I see more people swimming and laughing, finding comfort from the hot sun in the cool water. I smell food cooking on someone's barbecue. It's making my stomach rumble.

Ben catches up to me and tells me to bring the box further onto the beach. I pick it up and follow him.

"Hey! There he is!" A guy calls out. All he's wearing is a pair of blue striped swim shorts. Two girls and another guy turn to look at Ben. The girls are wearing their bikinis. One has short blonde hair and is wearing a striped hot pink and white bikini. The other has brown hair that is gathered atop her head. She is wearing a solid blue bikini that sparkles when the sun hits it just right. The other guy is wearing his red checkered swim shorts with a gray t-shirt. I stop with the box, my lunch, and my water still in my hands. The guy that saw Ben first gives him a handshake and pounds, and the blonde girl gives him a hug. I'm still standing with the stuff in my hands, just taking it in. The girl that gave Ben a hug saw me standing and staring. "Who's this?" she asks.

"Oh, I'm sorry," Ben says when he sees me standing holding the box and my stuff. Ben takes the box out of my hands and sets it down. "Guys, this is Jessica or Jess. Jess, this is my friend Dave," he points to the guy with the striped blue swim shorts.

"Jack," he points to the guy with the t-shirt and swim shorts.

"Becky," he points to the blonde.

"I work with them, and Liv is Jack's girlfriend."

I wave. All wave back except Becky. I don't think Becky knew I was coming.

"Did you bring the net?" Jack asks.

Ben grabs the box I was carrying and says, "Yep. In here." "Sweet! I'll help you set it up," Jack offers.

Liv follows Jack. Great. I'm alone with Dave and Becky. They are both staring at me. I wonder what they are thinking.

Then Dave walks up to me. "So, are you Ben's new girlfriend?"

"I wouldn't quite say girlfriend yet since we aren't dating," I reply.

"So you're not dating him?" Becky asks.

"No. We haven't gone out on a date yet," I clarify.

Dave wraps his arm around me. "Well, don't be shy. You are welcome here. Here, have a seat," as he gently guides me to sit on the bench at the picnic table.

"You want a beer?" Dave has one in his hands already.

"No, thanks," I said.

Becky sits on the opposite side of the table, watching me. Or more like judging me. I feel like I need a book to hide behind or I need to find something to do. I turn around and I see Jack, Ben, and Liv putting up a volleyball net. They are almost done.

Chapter 6

With the volleyball net up, they take a break and everyone is sitting at the picnic table eating their lunches. Becky and Dave are still sort of checking me out as I eat. I'm thankful that Ben is sitting next to me. I feel safe from his friends.

When Ben finishes done eating, he says, "Who's up for a game of beach ball volleyball?" I was afraid of that. The last time I played volleyball, I cracked my wrist by just hitting the volleyball. Plus, I'm not very good at this game. Well, the good news is, it's just a beach ball and a lot softer than a regular volleyball. I'll be ok if Ben is on my team.

"We'll do guys versus girls," Jack says.

Poo.

"We'll be gentlemen and let the ladies go first," Dave announces as he hands me the ball. I smirk as I roll the ball in my hands. I walk to my side of the net. Becky says, "You can serve first."

Great. I'm nervous. Everyone is watching me. I exhale. I can't hide and now I have to clear my head and ignore the eyes that are watching me. I throw the ball up in the air with my left hand, and I smack it over the net with my right. I did it! The game is on. The guys manage to get the ball back to our side. Liv and Becky bounce it off their hands onto the guys' side. Then Ben smacks it all the way over to me. I go to pound it up, but let it drop to the ground.

Oops.

The guys give each other high fives. Liv and Becky look at me, not mad, but not especially happy. I pick up the ball and toss it to the guys. They serve since they got the point. Jack hits the ball over the net. It's coming right at me. I bounce it off my hands.

Sweet!

Then Becky hits it up higher and Liv smacks it down on the other side of the net. She's good! The girls got us a point. Liv serves next. She throws the ball up in a swirl and smacks it to the guys. She obviously played volleyball in high school. The guys hit the ball between them then over the net to us. Becky runs to return it and smacks it back over. The ball hits Ben in the face.

Ooooh. That had to hurt.

Becky runs underneath the net to Ben. "I'm sorry. I'm so sorry, Ben," she yells frantically.

I go under the net to Ben, getting a closer look at the damage. Nothing too serious. Just a red mark on his forehead.

"Nice hit," he says.

"Thanks," Becky says, blushing.

I think Becky has a crush on Ben. Who wouldn't, really? We all go back to our positions. Dave says, "One point for each team."

Liv is going to serve again. She smacks it over to the guys.

We played until it was guys seven and girls five. I missed the ball a couple of times, but I was good at serving. The wind was starting to pick up. It was Ben's turn to serve. He throws the ball up into the air and smacks it. The ball was starting to go over the net when a breeze blows by. Since it was a beach ball, the breeze blows the ball out toward the water. Finally! I saw the opportunity to get into the water. I quickly take off my tank top and shorts and run towards the waves. The breeze is still blowing the ball away from the beach while it playfully floats on the water. I swim after it as fast as I could. I catch it! I turn around and I see all five of them on the edge of the beach. Their feet barely touching the water. There were also some other spectators watching me catch the ball. I wish I were a mermaid now. I would go under the water with the ball and swim away. Instead, I slowly swim back to the beach with the ball in my arm. I swim till I can touch the ground again, then I start walking out toward the sand.

"You're a fish!" says Ben.

Dave was staring at me with his mouth wide open. Apparently, I made an impression. Becky, however, had her arms crossed. When I looked at her, she turned and walked away. Jack and Liv followed. Ben followed them.

Dave puts his arm around me again and said, "I wouldn't pay any attention to Becky. I think she's just jealous. Where did you learn to swim like that?"

Ben turned around, walking backwards, waiting to hear my answer as well.

"I took swimming lessons when I was little then my dad took over. Every time we went camping next to a lake, my dad, my brother, and I would jump in and swim. My dad and I used to have swimming races. My mom saw my potential and put me on the swim team. I couldn't compete though because my parents didn't have the money to keep me on the team."

"Impressive," Dave says with his arm still around me.

From out of nowhere, Becky takes the ball from my arm. She runs back towards the water and turns back around saying, "I bet you can't take this ball away from me."

Liv shouts, "I bet I can!"

Everyone starts chasing. I smile then I start in on the chase. Ben ends up smacking the ball out of her hands, and the ball goes flying back in the water. Jack throws off his shirt and runs into the water to catch it. Ben peels his shirt off and exposes his pale white skin. He runs into the water with Jack. The rest of us stay on shore, watching while Jack and Ben wrestle for the ball. The ball pops out of their arms and goes flying into the air. The ball itself is almost out of air. It flies further out to the lake. My opportunity again to swim after it. Making a mad dash, I run into the water and dive into the lake. Ben and Jack are right behind me. I make sure they can't get past me. I grab hold of the ball and dive under water with it, so neither Jack nor Ben can get me or the ball. I swim under water for quite a while until I need to catch my breath. I pop my head back up to see where I'm at and where they're at. They are not far behind me. They must have seen me underwater. I start swimming for shore. By the time I'm able to touch the ground, Ben wraps his arms around me. I am still holding the ball, fighting to get away. Liv runs into the water, furiously splashing us while Ben keeps a firm hold on me. In an instant, Liv grabs the ball out of my hands before I had a chance to react.

"No!" I yell.

I watch Liv run out of the water and back on to the beach. Jack is not far behind, gaining ground until he is right behind her. He grabs her from behind. Liv shrieks as he lifts her off the ground. I don't know what happened after that because I realize Ben still has his arms wrapped around me, and my arms are crossing my body. My hands are holding Ben's arms. I'm enjoying his warm body, standing there in the cold water. I turn my head to look at him. Then I turn my body to face him. His arms are still holding me.

I look at Ben, and he teases, "You are hard to catch." I smile and blush.

"Can you float too?" he asks me.

"Sure. Watch."

Ben lets go of me, and I lay down in the water like there is nothing to it. I put my hands behind my head, showing off just a bit. I remark, "If I could, I would float all day like this. Just sleep. The problem is

I would float to the middle of the lake, and I would have a hard time getting back to shore."

I feel Ben's hands on my back and under my legs, holding me, guiding me. I get tingles down my spine from his touch. I feel him moving me in the water. I close my eyes.

"I wonder if this is what flying feels like," I muse with my eyes still shut. "I always imagined flying would be like swimming in the water except I could breathe freely."

Chapter 7

 woke up to Ben's soft voice, "Hey. I'm needed on shore. I have to start making supper." I pop my eyes open. Holy smokes! I wonder how long I've been sleeping. I feel like I could have continued sleeping and floating, with not a care in the world. I rub my eye with my right hand while I feel Ben grab my left hand. He leads me out of the water toward the picnic table. The sun is way in the west now. It's barely touching the trees. My stomach growls, reminding me it's time for dinner. I sit down next to the camp stove that someone brought for the occasion. It was already set up with a frying pan waiting for the food. Ben opens up the cooler he brought and digs out a couple of packages of hamburger patties. He turns on the stove and places the patties in the frying pan. The warm fire feels good. I'm in my wet bikini, the sun is going down, and the breeze is still blowing. I feel the goose bumps popping up on my skin. I shiver.

Ben must have noticed because he said, "I have my shirt down next to the lake that you can wear. I'll go get it."

He runs off towards the water to get his shirt, Jack's shirt, and my clothes. I slide closer to the stove, trying to get more heat from it. Ben drops my clothes and Jack's shirt next to the table and puts his button up shirt on me. It's a t-shirt. It doesn't cover up much. I'm still cold.

"Maybe I'll go to the car and grab my warm clothes," I say to Ben. "Actually, I need your help while I make these burgers."

"Oh, okay," I said. Moving around will help me warm up.

Ben moves the cooler closer to me and says, "Everything is in there: the tablecloth, buns, plates, condiments... Can you set the table?"

"I can do that," I said with a smile.

I look in the cooler. Wow! Ben thought of everything. He even thought of table clips to hold the tablecloth down on the table. I work around Ben as I put the table cloth down and set the clips on. Next, I take the package of plates, napkins, and box of forks and put them on the table. Next, I place the ketchup, mustard, pickles, and sliced cheese out for everyone. Wow! He even took the time to slice the onions and tomatoes, and shred the lettuce! I'm impressed that he worked so hard for this picnic. After I set everything on the table, Jack and Liv add chips. Then Becky brings out a big bowl of potato salad. Now I feel bad that I didn't bring anything. I could've brought the drinks. Then I see Dave bring a case of beer to the table. Never mind. Everything was taken care of. Just like Ben said.

Still chilly, I ask Ben, "Can I have your car keys so I can get my warm clothes?" Ben says, "Yeah, but I'll come with you. I have to use the restroom anyway."

I wait as he flips the burgers, grab his keys from the box I carried earlier, and grabs my clothes. He is very thoughtful. He puts my clothes under his arm so he can have a free hand, and that free hand grabs my free hand.

As we walk to the car, Ben says, "I have to admit. I don't want you to put your warm clothes on. You look pretty hot with your bikini and my shirt on."

I couldn't help but smile and blush. I couldn't think of anything to say other than, "Thank you."

He continues to hold my hand all the way to the car. I like it. He opens up the trunk and hands me my clothes. I have my clothes in one hand, and I grab my bag with the other.

"I'll meet you half-way," I say. "How about I put my shorts on and I leave my bikini top on with your shirt?"

Ben's eyes light up and he gives me a really big smile, "I like that idea."

I went into the restroom and take off my wet bottoms. All I really wanted to do was take off my wet bikini. I know I will warm up faster if I did that. I put my underwear and shorts back on. I feel better already. I take my sweatshirt out just in case and shove everything else in my bag. Oh, yes. My hair. My hair was still wet. It would dry faster if I let it down. I take the ponytail out and undo the twists that my mom put in. Ahh. I feel much better, but I smell like fish. I don't have anything to cure that. I walk out of the restroom with my bag over my shoulder. Ben turns and looks at me. His jaw drops.

"What?" I say.

"I said you looked hot before, but you look beautiful," he says.

I blush and start walking down the steps to the car.

Ben continues, "You look like you walked out of a magazine."

I looked at him quizzically. "I hope not a Cosmo or a porn magazine," I said.

"No. More like a fashion magazine. The way your brown hair is, and your shorts, and my shirt." I blush again.

I notice that Ben has his clothes in his hands now. He must've noticed that I was aware of that because he stopped looking at me and started up the steps to the restroom. I took this chance to look at myself in the mirror. Whoa. My hair did look pretty. I liked how my hair curled away from my face, and the hair in the back of my head was straight. My eyes need some work, though. I'm glad I brought my eye make-up. I quickly dig it out of my bag, and apply some eye shadow and eye liner.

I see Ben open the restroom door. I quickly slam my eye make-up kit shut and shove it in my bag. I turn around, put my bag in the trunk, and place my sweat shirt over my arm. Ben is right behind me. He is putting his wet shorts in the car. I take a good, long look at him. He's now wearing baggy, khaki shorts and a casual light blue shirt. I know I have to say something about his appearance since he complimented me. "That shirt really brings out your blue eyes," I say to him, and it really did. I glance at his face, looking to see if I can make him blush like how he makes me blush. All I saw was a smirk. I wonder what he is thinking. Ben wraps his arm around me as we walk back to the picnic table. I smile as I wrap my arm around his waist.

Chapter 8

$\mathcal{W}$e are still arm and arm when we get back to the picnic table. Everyone's head pops up when we show up. Ben automatically says, "Sorry you had to take over the cooking, Jack, but thanks."

"That's fine," Jacks says. "Looks like you were busy."

I sit down at the opposite end of the camp stove now and Ben sits down next to me, in between the stove and me. Both of us grab a paper plate and bun. Everyone else does the same as they sit down. Dave is sitting directly across from me, followed by Liv, then Becky. Jack puts the hamburger patties in the middle of the table and takes his spot in between Becky and Liv. We all grab a patty at the same time. We act like we are starving. I know I was. We dress our burgers, grab some chips, and scoop a big spoonful of potato salad.

"Want a beer?" Dave offers.

"No thanks," I tell him again.

"Do you not drink?" Dave asks.

"No," I answered.

"Is it because you are under-age?" asks Becky.

Ben shot a look at her.

"Yes. That is one of my reasons." I reply. "More reasons include: I don't like the taste of beer and my dad is an alcoholic. His drink is beer."

"I'm sorry," Dave says.

"Me too," says Ben.

No one talked as we ate. All you could hear were others in the distance playing, laughing, talking, and splashing around in the water.

Now that I'm sitting down away from the camp stove and closer to the trees, I'm getting cold again. The breeze is coming right out of the trees and out towards the water. I shiver. Ben sees me again and moves closer to me. This time our thighs and shoulders are touching. I'm getting the tingles again. I look and smile at him. He smiles back at me, and we keep eating.

"What's the deal?" Dave shouts out. "I thought you guys weren't dating, and how come you always get the cute ones?" Dave looks at Ben.

Both Ben and I stop eating.

"Yeah!" Becky pipes in. "I thought you liked me. That's why you invited me. Right?" Now I see Ben blush. Uh-oh. What's happening?

Dave continues, "When you guys got here, I asked her if you guys were dating and she said no."

Now *I'm* blushing, and I feel bad.

Ben chimes in, "That's because today was kind of our first date. We decided to go steady last week."

I stop blushing and shoot Ben a big, wide smile.

"But I thought you liked me," Becky says again.

Liv stands up and says, "Stop you guys! The reason I told Ben to invite you Becky because we thought you and Dave could be an item."

Dave and Becky look at each other across from Jack and Liv, then shake their heads. "Sorry, Becky," Liv said. Jack puts his hand on her shoulder, guiding her to sit back

down.

Jack pipes in, "Why do we care who's dating who? I thought we were here to celebrate and have fun." Everyone nods their heads and continues eating.

After a-while, Liv gets up and takes a Tupperware out of a box. She brings it to the table and opens the lid. We all peek inside. Red, white, and blue sugar cookies. Wow! Happy Independence Day! You could tell that Liv made them. We all grab a cookie and take a bite.

Jack says, "Liv, you've out done yourself again." Liv looks at Jack lovingly and she kisses him on the cheek. I couldn't help but admire and sigh at the gesture. It was a cute moment.

"Anyone wants some more?" Liv asks as she puts the Tupperware in front of each of us.

We all shake our heads.

"That was wonderful, Liv. Thank you," as Ben rubs his tummy.

Liv speaks next. "Thank you, Ben for inviting us all out and providing the meal." Everyone, including me, say, "Yeah. Thank you, Ben."

I look toward the lake, and can barely see the sun above the trees. It would be a couple of hours before the fireworks start. I pick up my plate and take it to the garbage. Everyone else follows. Dave puts his camp stove away, and I help Ben put the food back in his cooler.

Next, Dave brings out a guitar case. How cool! He sits down in the sand next to the picnic table. He gently lifts his guitar out of the case and starts tuning it. I watch closely as he handles his prized possession with care. Dave must have noticed I was watching. "Do you play?"

I answer, "No, but I would love to learn one day. I am going to school this fall to be a music teacher."

Everyone seemed impressed. Dave pats the dirt next to him, wanting me to sit beside him. "I'll teach you. It's not that hard."

I slip over next to him and he places the guitar in my lap. He then sits behind me and places my left hand on the neck. I look at Ben, and he is sitting on the sand across from us. Pinks, oranges, and yellows glow behind him from the sunset. He's smiling, watching me. In fact, I notice that he can't take his eyes off me. Dave guides my right hand over the body of the guitar, then softly touches my left hand and tells me to relax it. I try. All of a sudden, it's not that easy. Dave then places three of my fingers on the strings, making sure my thumb is behind the neck.

"Ok. Strum."

I strum the guitar with my right hand. It makes a chord.

"That is the F chord," Dave tells me.

I am curious. "Ok. Now are each individual strings notes?"

"Yeah," Dave replies. "From the top. E, A, G, D, B, E. But, you can find all the natural notes just on the first string."

I gently lay the guitar on my lap with the strings facing up. "Ok. Where's C?" I ask.

He shows me and I start plucking. C, C, G, G, A, A, G.

I stop and ask, "Where's F?" Dave shows me and I keep plucking. F, F, E, E, D, D, C. Everyone starts clapping, and they are all sitting in a circle now, watching us. It was just an easy tune: "Twinkle, Twinkle, Little Star." "You are a fast learner," Dave comments.

"I just have my notes memorized from playing piano," I offer.

A little embarrassed, I hand the guitar to Dave, stand up, and walk to where Ben is sitting and try to gracefully plop down next to him, hoping not to attract any attention. I turn around and admire the rich red and oranges as they begin to fade over the trees. I hear Dave strumming on the guitar. Before long, the sun is now down below the trees. It's getting dark fast. I still hear people on the beach talking, but they are winding down from a full day of fun. I'm looking through the trees. My favorite spot in the whole world is right through there. I bet the sunset would've looked pretty from that spot. I bet even more that watching the fireworks there, it would be romantic.

Ben interrupts my thoughts. "What are you looking at?" "Oh, sorry," I say. "Nothing really."

I couldn't help myself. I had to ask. "You want to go somewhere else and watch the fireworks? I know a place."

Without question, he gets up and starts gathering up his stuff.

"Where are you going?" Becky asks.

Ben hands me the box. "We are going somewhere else to watch the fireworks," he says.

Then he grabs the cooler and starts walking towards the car.

"We will see you later, buddy," Jack yells.

"Yeah. I'll see you guys back at work," Ben yells back over his shoulder.

I quickly say, "It was nice to meet you," and I start chasing after Ben.

We made it back to the car, we load up the trunk, and get in. Then Ben turns his head toward me and says, "Where are we going?"

I answer, "Okay. You have to get back on the road, and instead of turning right to get back on the interstate, turn left toward the dam." I've been here many times. I know this place like the back of my hand.

Ben starts the car and backs out of our parking spot. He gets on the road and turns left.

"Take the exit to go to the dam." He takes the exit.

"Instead of going down to the dam, go up to Cottonwood Area." Ben starts going uphill to Cottonwood. We see a lot of cars parked around the area and on both sides of the narrow street.

"See if you can find a parking spot next to the restrooms over there," as I point across the way. Ben drives around slowly since there are so many people. Luckily, he finds a parking spot across from the restrooms. I get out, and I know he can feel my excitement. I cannot hold it in. I run across the road to the campsite that is on the way to our spot. I know Ben is right behind me so I reach my hand around, and he grabs it. It's dark now. I'm hoping no one is sitting where I want to be. I run into the trees.

"Where are we going?" Ben asks.

"You'll see," I tease.

Finally. I notice a familiar rock. "Look there's turtle rock!" I point to a big boulder with a long rock sticking out of it, making it look like the head of a turtle coming out of its shell. I sprint to another rock that is long with a hole in the middle of it. I run behind it and stick my face through the hole.

Ben giggles. "What do you call this rock?"

"I call it chimney rock," I answer.

Ben gets his phone out of his pocket and takes a picture of me. I begin to walk closer to the edge of the cliff. I put my hand on another big boulder. "I call this rock lover's rock because of all the couples that have signed their names on it."

Ben rubs his hand over it, looking at the hearts, initials, and names. I carefully walk around lover's rock to the edge. I sit down with my back resting on the rock. It makes a perfect chair. Ben carefully walks around the other side and sits comfortably down next to me.

"This is amazing!" He is in awe.

We see the lights of boats dotted all over the lake, waiting for the show. We see people lining the shores, sitting in their chairs and blankets. Everyone is waiting for a spectacular fireworks show.

"This is an amazing spot to watch the fireworks," he announces.

"I think so too," I say. "This is my first time watching fireworks here." "How did you know about this place?" he asks.

I look to my right. "My family likes to camp over there. Every time we do, I walk through the trees and up the hill to get here. I usually read, write in a journal, or just watch people and listen."

I turn to look at him, and his eyes are dancing with excitement as he gives me a big grin. I look back out toward the lake. I take a deep breath of the cool, fresh air. I see the moon and boat lights dancing on the water. Surprisingly, I don't hear any people noises or voices, except for the crickets. I look at my toes now. I'm not sure what else to say, and that's okay for now because I enjoy having Ben next to me in all this quietness. It wasn't quiet for long, however, because soon the whistling and cracking and booming of the fireworks began.

I love the chandelier ones. "So pretty," I say.

"You sure are."

"What?" I turn to look at him, and he was right there, a couple of inches away, looking back at me. He leans in closer. I think he's going to do what I think he's doing. I'm frozen, and I shut my eyes. His lips touch mine. They are soft and gentle. I'm still frozen. He leans back on lover's rock, taking a good, long look at me. I'm still frozen. I haven't moved. My mind is even frozen.

"Was that okay?" he asks.

I shake my head, trying to thaw my mind, then nod. "Yeah. It was fine."

I feel embarrassed. I think that I might have hurt his feelings. I have to tell him the truth.

"Ben, that was my first kiss. I'm sorry. I didn't know what to do or how to act."

Ben shoots back a look of astonishment. "But you have had boyfriends before right? Or gone on dates, haven't you?"

I shake my head yes.

"But they've never kissed you?"

I shook my head no, then I said, "I wouldn't let them. I wanted my first kiss to be special. Yes, they have all tried to kiss me, but I would push them away."

Ben looks at his toes. "Well, I hope I didn't ruin your first kiss." "You didn't," I said… a little louder than I wanted to.

I lower my voice. "This is actually the most romantic date I've ever been on. Other guys just take me to a movie. I've never even been out to eat with a guy. I went to one guy's house once, but all he wanted to do was get in my pants. He had more moves than an octopus."

Ben kind of giggles at that remark. "I'm sorry," he says. "There are creeps out there, but I hope you don't think I am one of them. Because I'm not."

"You most definitely are not," I said quickly. "Honestly, Ben, you are the most gentlemanly guy I know. You are very considerate of my feelings and of others. In fact, when I heard you were going out with that senior when I was junior, I said to myself, 'Ben can do so much better than her'. I knew who she was and how she acted. I was pretty upset about it. I think it was because I also had a little crush on you. All the girls in that school did."

I blush. Telling secrets can be embarrassing.

I see Ben smile and relax against the rock again, watching the fireworks. I move closer to Ben and look up at the bursting colors in the dark sky.

Chapter 9

After we watch the fireworks for a-while, Ben opens up, "I kind of had a crush on you, too, for a-while. You were cute as a freshman, and each year, you grew and matured. I started finding myself attracted to you. I even asked your friend, Rick, about you. He told me you were seeing someone else, and that he had a thing for you, too."

I was taken aback. *Ewww*, I thought. I didn't say a word. I let Ben continue.

"I have gone on dates with other girls, but they wanted all the attention and talked a lot. You don't talk much."

I blush.

He's right. I've never been a talker. I almost got held back in kindergarten for not talking. "I remember," he trails off. "I remember when that guy was trying to flirt with you at that track meet, and I told you he was. You nodded your head saying, 'I know.' I was confused. I didn't know if you were being rude, if you just didn't care, or if that happened to you a lot. Now, listening to you, I know that you get hit on by guys a lot."

I nod my head knowing that Ben was spot on. I didn't even blush. I honestly just wanted to hide away from every man. And now, I'm working at a place with a bunch of men. I didn't like it, but it was a job to help pay for college. Plus, my dad helped me get the job.

"Right now," Ben continues, "I feel grateful that you came with me today. Thank you." I look deeply into his eyes and smile. I almost feel like crying because a man actually

wanted to go out with me because he liked me for me and not for how I look.

The fireworks are now really going strong, one right after the other at a furious rate. It must be the finale. I can't believe it's been an hour already. Ben and I carefully walk back around lover's rock. When we reach the other side, we take each other's hand. We walk side by side through the trees back to the car. We hear people wrapping things up. Everyone seems to be in a rush to get to bed or head back home. Ben and I take our time. We reach the campsite next to the restrooms, and I pause, "I better use the bathroom before we leave."

"That sounds like a good idea."

I head into the women's side and Ben walks around to the men's side. We both happen to walk out at the same time, and we grab each other's hand again, even though we are just walking across the road to his car. Ben opens the passenger side for me and helps me in. He shuts the door behind. I watch him walk around the car to the driver's side as I snap my seat belt shut. He gets in the car and starts it up. He finishes driving around the circle to get back to the road. We take our place in line, waiting our turn to get on the main road. As we wait, he lays his hand on the console with his palm facing up. I smile and take his hand. Neither of us says a word. We just listen to the radio. We finally get back on the interstate and start picking up speed. I fall asleep while holding Ben's hand.

I wake up when Ben gently lets go of my hand. I look out my window. My house is right there. I'm home already. He gets out and walks around the car to open the door for me. He helps me out, and we walk to the back of his car and he opens the trunk to get my stuff.

He hands me my lunch box and water, then carries my bag as we walk up the stairs onto the deck. He puts my bag down, takes my lunch box and water and sits it down next to my bag. At that moment, Ben gently puts his hands on my neck under my hair and leans in. His lips take hold of my bottom lip. I automatically take hold of his top lip. This lasts for a few minutes. After we end, I find my hands wrapped around his neck. I gently let go.

"Good night, Jess" Ben says.

"Good night, Ben" I say, mesmerized by what just took place.

Ben walks back down the stairs to his car. I watch him start the engine and drive away. I pause a minute and take a big sigh. I pick up my lunch box, water, and bag. I open the porch door and walk across the porch to the sliding glass door. I tiptoe into the house and shut off the porch light. It was nice that my parents left the light on for me. I slowly shut the door and drop my stuff next to it. I walk like a zombie to my bedroom and plop myself on my bed. Then I realize, "Oh, man. I still have his shirt on." I shrug and sniff his shirt. I smile and fall asleep.

My alarm wakes me with that annoying buzzing and I immediately slam the snooze button. It can't be time to wake up already. I'm still tired, but I have to go to work. I switch the snooze to off and muster the energy to get out of bed. I get up like a zombie. As slow as I am this morning, I won't have to time to take a shower, dry my hair, get ready, eat breakfast, and make my lunch. I decide to skip the shower and I start taking off Ben's shirt, my bikini top, and my shorts. I put on clean undergarments, a casual tee, jeans, socks, and my steel toed shoes. I also make sure I put deodorant and perfume on to hopefully keep the fishy smell at bay. I leave my hair alone. It still looks good with the curls. I make my way out of my room and into the kitchen.

My mom is the first to speak. "Did you have fun yesterday?" "Yeah," I answer. I'm still not quite awake.

I walk over to the kitchen counter and start making my breakfast. My mom can see I'm still tired. "Maybe you can tell me about yesterday later today after work."

I nod my head, yes.

I eat my breakfast, make my lunch, and brush my teeth. I slowly walk outside to the garage. I get into the car and blare my music so it can keep me awake on the drive in. I park in my usual parking spot, walk in and say hi to the receptionist, clock in, and walk to my desk. I see there are papers on my desk ready for me to enter in from the night crew. I sign in to my computer. My boss notices how tired I am because she asks, "Late night last night, watching the fireworks?"

I nod my head.

"You could've called in," she said.

"No, I'll be fine," I said.

After all, my job doesn't require a lot of energy. All I do is enter data into the computer, scan papers, and then shred them. If I had to do more than that and interact with people, I would've called in. I can do this job tired. I can practically do it with my eyes closed.

Morning speeds by pretty fast. I clock out and get my lunch box out. I start eating my sandwich and begin thinking about Ben. I can't stop smiling and I know I look kind of guilty, but I don't care. No one had a night like I did, so I'm the lucky one.

The afternoon drags on. I keep counting the hours until it's time to clock out. I am really tired. I keep yawning and tiny tears are streaming down my face. At 3 o'clock, my phone dings. Good thing I'm just standing at the scanner, doing nothing more than watching the paper go in the machine, then back out.

Ben: How is your day going?

Me: I'm tired, other than ok.

Ben: Sorry u r tired. U have to work today?

Me: Yeah. I'm off in a couple of hours.

Ben: I'm off this week. Can I come see you at work tomorrow or
      Friday?

I smile. Yeah, sure. Any day works. I'm not an important person here, so I'm sure they won't mind.

Ben: I'm sure u r important otherwise they wouldn't have hired u.

I smile. The stack of papers I put in the scanner is now done. I pick them up and put them back in the box. I go to my computer and put the scanned file in the work folder. I go back to the box and start putting papers in the shredder, a little bit at a time. My phone dings again.

Ben: Can I bring you a lunch on Friday?

Me: Yeah. That would be great.

Ben: When is your lunch hour?

Me: Typically noon.

Ben: I'll c u on Friday. And get some sleep.

Me: I will. C u on Friday!

For a few minutes, I feel energized and up, now that I talked to Ben. *Sigh* And only 15 minutes have gone by.

By the time 5 o'clock hits on the dot, I log out of my computer, gather up my purse and lunch box, clock out, and head home. I blare my music on the way home again so I can stay awake. When I get home, I tell my mom not to bother making supper for me. I jump into the shower, put on my jammies, and snuggle into bed for a nice long sleep.

Chapter 10

On Friday morning, I wake up in a really good mood because Ben is coming to see me today. I do my normal routine except make my lunch. On the way to work, I blast my music and sing in the car. I greet everyone I come in contact with as I walk toward the clock-in computer and to my desk.

"You seem rather happy this Friday," my boss notices.

"Yeah. By the way, I'm having a visitor today. Is that okay?" I ask.

"That's fine. Is this visitor a boy?" she asks teasingly.

I smile, "Yes, it's a boy."

Lunch hour couldn't come any faster. Then 15 minutes before noon, there is a knock on the side of the door. I look up and there's Ben, already.

"I'm a little early. I hope that's okay."

"That's fine," I said.

Luckily, I was at my desk entering data and filing instead of standing at the scanner or shredder. I look at my boss, and my boss is smiling, with her eyes wide open.

She says, "Show him around. Give him a tour. Then you can clock out and have lunch." I give her a big smile and say, "Thanks." I turn to Ben. "Let me log out of my computer first."

I stand up and guide Ben toward the mechanic's shop. I'm glad he wore sensible shoes and not sandals. He introduced himself to some guys and asked them some questions. After that, I took him to the machine shop. He was quite interested with the machines he saw. I didn't know anything about them, so I'm glad he did. Then I walked him to the welding shop.

My dad is in town today, so I walk around a bit with Ben until I find him. Jokingly, I say, "Look who showed up for a tour today."

"Oh, well, hi," my dad offers.

Ben shakes his hand. "This is a cool place. Jess said that you work here, too. Are your hours okay?"

My dad gets to talking with Ben, and both of them engage in what I call "guy talk" for a bit. I kind of space out, not really listening to the conversation. I'm just glad they had something in common to talk about. I take my phone out of my pocket and look at the time. "I need to clock out," I said.

My dad says, "Me too. Lunch time."

Ben asks suddenly, "I was going to take Jess out for lunch. Want to come with us?"

My dad, being my dad, asks, "Where are we going?"

Ben shrugs, "Where ever you would like to eat?"

"I like the Chinese buffet down the way," my dad suggests.

My face lightens up. "I haven't eaten there in a long time," I add.

"I'll drive," my dad says.

I follow Dad and Ben out to my dad's car. I tell Ben he can have the front seat, and I can sit in the back. "Are you sure?" Ben asks.

"I'm sure."

We all climb in, and Dad drives us to the buffet.

As we walk in, the hostess walks us to our seats and asks what we want to drink. My dad and I both ask for hot tea and water. Ben asks for Mountain Dew. Then we head to the buffet and grab our food. I'm the first one back to the table. I have my normal fried rice, green beans, pork-on-a-stick, sweet-n-sour pork, beef and broccoli, and an egg roll. Then Ben comes back with his food. The typical rice and meat assortment. My dad is the last to arrive at the table, balancing two plates in his hands. Of course, my dad has the oysters, fish, sushi, and whatever else that looks like a good catch to him.

"Whoa!" Ben says as he looks at Dad's plate. "I didn't realize you can eat that."

I pipe in and say, "Yeah, that's our Asian side. My dad is half, and I'm a quarter." "I didn't know that," Ben says in amazement. "You don't really look it."

I look at him, and he is looking at me. "Ok. Yeah. I see it now. It's in your eyes." I smile.

I wish lunch time was longer. I didn't want to go back to work. I wanted to stay and hang out with Ben. There wasn't much one on one conversation since my dad was there, but that was okay. The fact that my dad likes him is a good thing. It's just that I wanted some one-on-one time with Ben with no one else around. Someday, hopefully. And especially before the summer ends.

Ben pays for our lunch. "That's a nice boy," Dad says to me as we watch Ben pay the cashier.

I nod my head. "I like him."

Dad drives us back to M&K Constructing and parks in his spot. "Thanks for lunch," Dad says, then shakes Ben's hand. "I'll see you some other time, hopefully."

Ben smiles.

Dad walks back into the welding shop. Ben and I hold hands as we walk back into the main building where I clock in. Once inside, we both turn toward each other and hug. I love the way he smells. Ben squeezes my hand and says, "I'll call you later."

I smile, "K."

I drag myself to the computer to clock in. When is later? Tonight? Tomorrow? Sunday?

Next week? Poo. When am I going to have an actual date? I clock in and start heading upstairs to the attic to get another box of papers to scan and shred. Four hours till I get to go home. I'm going to challenge myself to scan and shred the entire box of papers before I go just to keep my mind off of Ben and wondering about our next date.

It's ten till five. I have a stack of papers left to scan and shred. Can I do it? I end up staying five minutes longer, but I got the box done. I carry the box back up the stairs to the attic. Only hundreds more left to do. I go back downstairs to log out of my computer and grab my purse. As I'm clocking out, my phone vibrates. It's Ben! His "later" means as soon as I get off work.

"Hey!" I answer.

"Are you off work?" Ben asks.

"Yeah. I just clocked out and I'm heading out the door."

"I hope I didn't make you stay late," he says. I can hear his sincerity.

"No. I just wanted to finish a box before I left for the weekend," I said as I walk out the door. The receptionist is already gone.

"That's good. I was hoping to take you out to eat before I head back to work. I'm going to be working for like two weeks straight, and I want to take you on a proper date before I do that."

"Why are you working two weeks straight?" I ask as I unlock my car. I hope he doesn't pick up on my disappointment.

"I kind of added my weekends off to my one week that I just had off. If that makes sense."

"Yeah," I said still disappointed, getting into the car. "Makes sense to me. So when do you want to do the date?" I switch my disappointment to excitement. I turn the car on and immediately turn down the volume on my radio, so I can hear Ben.

"I was hoping tomorrow night. If that's okay? I hope you don't have plans already."

"I don't," I said quickly. I start backing out of the parking lot and drive towards the main road to head home.

"You still there?" he asks.

"Yeah, sorry. I'm on my way home," I answer.

"Should I let you go?"

"No. I'm fine now. Just had to concentrate for a little bit. Shall I meet you somewhere tomorrow?" I ask, trying to keep on subject.

"No. I'll pick you up around 5:30. We'll go out to eat, and dress semi-nice." Now, I'm excited. "Oooh. Sounds fancy," I say playfully. "Not that fancy. Just nice pants and shirt," he says.

"How about a skirt or a simple dress? Is that ok?" I ask.

"That works too. So I guess I'll see you tomorrow at 5:30, and drive carefully." He is so thoughtful.

"I will," I say.

It felt like I was getting ready for the prom. It basically took me all day to get ready for the date: I waxed, put a face mask on to clean my pores, did my toenails and fingernails, showered, put my hair in curlers, chose an outfit, took the curlers out, put on my make-up, and selected jewelry. My toenails and fingernails are painted with silver sparkles under a clear coat. I select a decent night-time outfit: a knee-high black layered skirt with a casual pink tank top and a white undershirt. I take the stole from my prom dress to wrap around my shoulders to keep me warm from the summer night air. My hair is curly like a poodle. I'm wearing my silver and black long earrings that I also wore to prom, a silver heart necklace, and a silver and black ring. To complete the ensemble, I'm wearing black, high-heeled, sandals. I'm taking my time getting ready. I'm fixing my curls and adding a white flower in my hair when I hear a knock at the door.

"Hi," my mom says as she opens the door for Ben. "I think she is almost ready. Let me go check."

My mom comes in my room and says, "Ben is here."

"I know," I said. "I need help with this curl. It won't stay."

My mom picks up a bobby pin and places the curl where it should be and hides the pin really well.

"Thanks, Mom," I say. I look at myself one more time in the mirror, "Am I overdressed?" "You look really pretty," my mom assures me. "Ben is waiting on you."

I sigh and head out of my bedroom. Ben is sitting at the dining room table as I walk out. He sees me and smiles. "You look pretty."

I know I heard it from my mom, but when Ben said it, I blushed. "Thanks."

He offers his arm to me. I was overwhelmed with how much of a gentleman he was. I take his hand and we head out the door.

"You guys have fun," my mom says.

We both turn and wave. We head down the stairs, and Ben helps me in his car. Off to town we go.

Chapter 11

$\mathcal{W}$e show up at a 1920s restaurant called *Ritzy & Spiffy*. I have never been here before.

We walk in, hand in hand, and Ben motions to the hostess. "Reservation for Ben," he says.

The hostess looks in her book. "Oh, yes. For two. Right this way."

We follow the hostess as she navigates through the restaurant. The place is really classy with chandeliers that look like they came from the 20s, tables and chairs, and booths, with candles on every table. The restaurant also has red carpeting and tassels hanging from every doorway. The hostess sits us down at a booth.

Our table looks different from the others. On our table, there are some red roses with baby's breath in them, a red candle, and a card with my name on it. I look at Ben, surprised. "How did you do this?"

Ben and the hostess smile at each other.

"I hope this didn't take too much trouble and money," I continue.

"It was worth it," Ben said. "You said you have never gone out to eat with a guy before, so I want to make it special for you."

I'm still amazed because he listened and remembered what I said a few days ago. I lean over and whisper in his ear, "I will never forget this."

"Open the card," he says. He's excited and a little impatient.

I open the red envelope and pull out the card. The front of the card has a picture of a rose, and it reads *I have a Special Message.* I open the card and the message reads, *Love is thinking about someone else more times in a day than you think about yourself. Can you guess who I'm thinking about?* In Ben's hand writing, underneath the message, it read **I hope you feel the same way. Ben.** I close the card and put it back down on the table. I look up at Ben and smile. "I think about you a lot, too." I reach my hand across the table and gently take hold of his hand.

The waitress shows up a minute or two later and asks what we want to drink. Ben speaks up before I say anything, "We will have two glasses of red Syrah." Then I add, "With water, please."

After the waitress hands us our menus and leaves, I ask Ben, "What is red Syrah?" "It's a red wine. I just want you to try it."

I sigh, feeling a little uptight.

It's just one glass, and I'm at a public place and not somebody else's house. I'll be fine. Is it sad that I can't fully trust Ben yet? Even though he is different than the other guys I have been with. He is a guy, and I am a girl. I have been educated on the dangers of alcohol, parties, and men and women. I can't think too much. I just need to enjoy myself.

Ben notices that I'm talking to myself and asks, "Are you okay?"

"I'm okay. Just thinking," I say, holding back on telling him what was on my mind.

"About what?" he pushes. Like Kendra.

"Nothing important. Have you been here before?" I try to change the subject.

"A couple of times with friends, and honestly, I've been here with a date or two." "It is a nice place," I say, trying not to feel resentful.

Our waitress shows up with our wine. Ben automatically takes a sip, and I watch. He sets his glass down and looks at me. I bring my glass to my lips and take a sip. Wow! This is good wine. It's so sweet and smooth. "It's good," I tell Ben. I take another sip.

Ben smiles, "I'm glad you like it."

Simultaneously, we look down at our menus. The food here is expensive. As I scan the entrees, I wonder what is the cheapest, yet good. I'm looking at the steaks. The cheapest steak, of course, is the sirloin. Maybe I'll just stick to a salad.

"Get anything you want," Ben says, as if reading my thoughts.

"The food here is expensive though," I reply.

Ben has already bought me flowers, and roses are not cheap, a card, and now paying for my wine. I'm thinking I'll just get a sirloin. I read what comes with my steak: soup or salad, bread, and a choice of one side. I think I'll have a salad and garlic mashed potatoes to go with my steak.

The waitress comes back, "Would you like any appetizers this evening?" Ben glances over at me and asks, "Stuffed mushrooms ok?"

I make a funny face and shake my head no. I have never liked mushrooms.

"Some fonduta then," Ben says to the waitress.

"Okay. I will put that in right away. Are you ready to order your meal?" I nod my head yes.

Ben said, "Go for it."

I order what I want.

Ben orders a t-bone with a salad and a loaded baked potato.

We sat quietly for a few minutes, but it wasn't uncomfortable. I have been wondering something, though, and I really want to know the answer. So I ask Ben, "How many girlfriends have you had? Overall. Including high school and possibly elementary school."

"Do you really want to know?" Ben answers me with a question. Not good in my opinion.

I nod my head yes.

"Twelve."

I nod my head again. He is an experienced guy, which is okay, but then I wonder. On the one hand, being experienced could mean he knows how to charm a lady and get her to do what he wants. On the other hand, Ben is good-looking and there could have been girls asking him out, so I find myself needing more information.

"How many serious relationships have you had?" I ask.

"Does it worry you that I have dated a lot of girls?" Ben answers me with a question again!

I didn't flinch. I was waiting for him to answer my question.

Finally, he says, "One."

I think to myself that that was a good answer. I feel relieved, but then I see sadness in his eyes. "What happened?" I ask.

"I don't know. I guess she didn't want me."

For some reason, that answer just didn't make any sense to me. "Are you sure that was it?"

"I don't know what happened. I really liked her. Actually, I loved her. I was going to ask her to move in with me after college. I did a lot for her. I thought I was there for her. Then she said she didn't want to see me anymore. She said she met another guy and started dating him. I didn't know if that was true, or if she just wanted me gone." Ben was looking at the floor, looking like a wounded dog.

My heart went to him. I could tell she really hurt him, whoever she was. "How long were you dating her? Then I corrected myself. "I mean, seeing her?"

"I met her when I first started college. She really caught my eye. I had to know who she was. I wanted to know everything about her. I thought she was "the one". We dated throughout our first two years of college. We were getting ready to graduate with our Associates when she dumped me."

"I'm sorry, Ben. What about the other eleven girls?"

Ben shrugs. "Just girls I thought were cute and took on dates a couple of times. They didn't last long. A couple of them actually asked me out."

"Do I have to remind you that you *are* pretty cute?" I ask, trying to get him to crack a smile.

That moment, Ben actually blushed.

Then he turned the tables. "What about that guy you were seeing when I asked Rick about you? How long were you with him?"

"I was only talking to him for three months. It was a long distance relationship, so of course it didn't last long. He was quite serious about me, though. He wanted us to go to college together. Then we were going to get married and he was going to buy a ranch with cows and we would have five kids. He had it all figured out, at least in his mind."

"Wow. I bet you broke his heart," Ben said, speaking with experience.

"I really don't know because the phone calls became less and less. When I visited him after the three months, I hardly recognized him. I don't know. Something changed. I wasn't heart broken. It just wasn't meant to be."

"Have you ever had your heart broken?" Ben presses me for an answer.

I shake my head no. "Luckily. Not even a family member death. I will be heart broken when my kitty dies though. I've had her since I was seven."

Ben chuckles. "I remember you telling me about your kitty at track practice that one day. I agreed with you about cats. They are easy to take care of."

I give a short laugh and nod my head an agreement. "I remember that, too." "I will have to see your kitty one day since she means so much to you."

I quickly add in, "She's shy toward strangers. If I'm around, she should be okay." "What's her name?" Ben had to ask, and I have a silly name for her. Ben is going to

laugh at me.

"Sbabys," I said quietly.

"What?" Ben leans in, trying to hear me.

"Sbabys," I said a little louder.

"Sbabys," he repeats with amusement. "That's original."

Thank goodness the food showed up. I didn't want to get any more embarrassed than I already was. Besides, I was hungry. Ben and I eat quietly, but it wasn't weird. Every now and then, I noticed him watching me eat. I blushed the first two times, then I began smiling at him.

Am I being a pig? Do I have food on my face? Did I smear my make-up? I excuse myself to use the restroom to have a look. Once I find the restroom, I have a quick look at myself. Everything is in order. What is he looking at?

When I get back from the restroom, Ben leans toward me and asks, "Did I tell you how pretty you look tonight?"

So that's why he keeps looking at me. I blush. Still blushing. Is the red in my face gone yet? Now I'm getting hot. I may need to excuse myself again.

Instead, the waitress came back, which was a good reason for me to stop blushing. "Are you two done with your plates?"

Ben and I say yes at the same time. We both look at each other and smile.

"I'll be right back." She takes our plates and leave.

Ben and I keep looking at each other, smiling. He makes it so easy to smile. I wonder what in the world is going on in that cute head of his. The waitress comes back with a chocolate lava cake and two forks. Okay. Ben found my weak spot. I look at him with amazement. "Oh. I love …." I almost said 'I love you'. No. I don't want to do that yet. I quickly say, "Chocolate! I love chocolate!" I blush. *Don't blush!* He might think I was going to say, "I love you." Not yet. We both dig in to the cake. I savor every bite. Yum! Each one better than the one before!

The silky chocolate melts in my mouth and rides smoothly down my throat. After we devour the cake, I gulp down the rest of my water. The waitress comes with the check and hands it to Ben. He takes out his card while the waitress is there so she can take it and run it right away.

"Now what would you like to do?" Ben asks me.

I'm surprised by his question and shrug my shoulders. "Let's not spend any more money tonight. Maybe a walk."

He's open to it. "Where shall we go for a walk?" Slowly, I answer, "Maybe around the town pond." "That sounds great."

The waitress comes back with the receipt and Ben's card. He finishes up the transaction and looks toward me. "Ready?"

I stand up to put my stole around my shoulders. Ben is there to help. I grab my flowers and the card with Ben at my side, we walk to his car.

Chapter 12

We get to the town pond and Ben parks his car, but he doesn't turn it off. The engine is idling and the classic rock station is playing in the background. To make things even a little more uncomfortable, a slow love song is playing. We sit in the car for a while, not talking. I didn't want anything to happen. I haven't set any boundaries yet. I don't know how far he has gotten with other girls. He certainly knows how to kiss. I press the pause button in my head and summon my memory to that time when we kissed on the 4th of July. You could say, I saw fireworks that night, like you wouldn't believe. I lick my lips thinking about it. Ben reaches over and takes hold of my hand. He's rubbing my hand. Now, I am scared again. Well, I either flight or fight. I let go of Ben's hand and got out of the car. I am walking down the sidewalk that is next to the pond. I put my stole up around my shoulders because the night breeze is cooler than I thought it would be. I hear frogs croaking and belting out sounds and crickets chirping all around me, while my high heels clap and slap with them every step I take. I hear the car turn off and then the car door shut. Next I hear the familiar chirp of his car as Ben locks it. In an instant, he is right next to me. He sure does run quietly.

I'm still thinking about what could have happened in the car if I hadn't gotten out. I'm not ready for anything physical and don't plan on it until I'm married.

"What's wrong?" His tone is serious.

I'm not going to be silent this time. "Sorry. I don't really know you yet, and I'm not ready for ..." My voice trails off, searching the right words to say for what I mean.

Ben realizes what I'm trying to say. "No! I'm not planning on doing anything like that until I know you well enough, too."

"Honestly?" I ask.

"Cross my heart. I promise I won't be like 'octopus man'."

I giggle. I feel relieved. I still have questions though. He has been with 12 girls. "What about the other girls you've dated?"

Ben hangs his head. "I knew I was going to have to answer this. Just didn't know I it was going to be this soon."

His comment gives away his answer. Yes, he has.

Now I have to ask, "How many?"

"Two."

"I'm assuming with the girl you loved."

Ben nods his head.

"And?"

"Another girl I wasn't planning on," he said. "We were partying and got drunk."

I notice guilt on his face. I'm actually glad there was guilt. "Any kids I need to know about?" I ask, knowing that's what happens afterwards.

"No!" He said quickly and loudly. "No, I made sure that wasn't going to happen." I nod my head.

We walk quietly for a while. I feel better knowing Sung Ben's history. It gives me perspective. "Since we are on the subject," Ben says, "how do you feel about it?" "Hmmm." I had to think about what he was trying to ask.

Ben asks again, "When do you feel that it's ok to...?"

I now know what he is trying to ask and I cut him off. "When me and my guy both have rings on our fingers and have signed our names on a certificate."

Ben lifts his eyebrows. "Not till after marriage?"

"Yes," I say firmly.

I feel like I have to tell him the reasons why I feel this way, so he can understand where I'm coming from. I start with an example. "For example, Kendra's older sister. She fell in love, got engaged, then got pregnant and he left her. He thought, 'if I just give her ring, she will do it with me, then I don't have to see her again'. Now, she's raising a baby by herself."

I look for any reaction from Ben. He says nothing. Not even a facial expression. I keep going, "Plus, wearing a white dress on a wedding day means a woman is pure. At least, that's what it meant back in the day. Now a days, it's just a fashion. When I walk the down aisle, I actually want to wear something that means I'm pure until that night. I guess I'm old fashion. That's what the guys in my high school didn't understand. I don't want to be their girlfriend right away. I want to date first before I decide."

Ben is still silent. I will stop talking. Maybe I will give him a chance to say something. At this point, I am very interested in his opinion. He lets go of my hand and walks toward the water. He stops at the water's edge and looks up at the moon. I stop walking and watch him for a good long minute. I wonder if I hurt his feelings. I don't really want to say sorry for something I believe in. I walk up next to him by the water. I take a long look out at the water.

"Look, if I said something that you don't agree with, then this relationship may not work." I said it straight forward. I might as well end it before hearts get broken.

I look at Ben, and he is still silent. What in the world is he thinking? Why won't he talk to me? I turn back toward the water. I don't know if

I should go or stand here with him. I would hold his hand but both of them are in his pockets. I study Ben's face. He's staring up at the moon.

After the awkward silence he finally asked a question that I didn't see coming. "Do you go to church?"

"I do. Every Sunday when we are not on vacation and Wednesdays for Bible class." "I wondered," he said.

Now I'm wondering what he is thinking. I have an idea. "I'm going to church tomorrow morning if you want to come. My mom, brother, and I go."

"Your dad doesn't go?" Ben asks.

"My dad has never come to church with us. I don't know why. I've never asked." Ben is still staring up at the moon.

"I've never dated a believer before," he says. "Yeah. I'll give church a try."

He finally looks at me again and smiles. He takes his hand out of his pocket, grabs my hand, and we continue our walk on the sidewalk around the pond.

That night we learned so much about each other. We talked about our families, where we were from, what we did growing up, and what our families did for fun. "I would love to meet your family," I say.

"Someday, hopefully."

We walked the circle around the pond and back to the car.

"I think I better take you home now," he says as he opens the passenger door. I smile back at him.

Ben turns on the car and turns up the heater. It was chilly for a summer night, but I managed to stay warm with my stole and Ben's warm body.

It was a quiet ride home. We held each other's hand, rubbing our thumbs together. When we get back to my house, Ben helps me out of the car and get my roses. This time, he walks me all the way into the house. He puts the roses and my card on the counter, and then he puts his hands on my hips. He looks directly into my eyes.

"What time should I be here tomorrow?"

"We leave for church at 8:15. We go to Bible class first and Worship begins at 10:00. If you want, I can wait for you here and we can leave at 9:30 for Worship," I offer.

"No. I'll come to Bible class with you guys. I need to learn about the Bible."

I smile wide. Ben then kisses me gently, yet passionately. I reciprocate the action. He lets go of me and leaves. I watch him drive away through the window. I turn around, head to my room, and get ready for bed.

Chapter 13

I wake up with Sbabys rubbing on me and purring. I smile and pet her. Besides Ben, she is the only one who can make me smile in the morning. Sunday. I have to get myself ready. I kiss Sbabys and get out of bed. I make my bed with the cat still on it. She maneuvers around where the bedspread goes, and does it very well! In the end, the bed is made and she never had to jump off! I check out hair in the mirror and see that it's still curly from last night, just a bit looser. I think it this way for church. I change into my church clothes, which today is my white layered skirt and a striped purple, blue, green, and white t-shirt with a white undershirt. I will get back to my make-up after breakfast.

Dad is already up when I walk into the kitchen to get a bowl of corn flakes.

"Want an egg?" he asks.

"Sure."

I eat my cornflakes while Dad makes my egg. When he gets done, he hands it to me and adds, "Want toast?"

"No, I'll just have bread." I get up from the table and get my own piece of bread to eat with my egg.

"I forget you are weird like that," he said as I sit back at the table.

My mom comes out of her room wearing her church clothes. "I made you an egg," my dad tells her.

"Thanks," she says.

She makes a piece of toast to go with her egg and takes her seat at the table. She wastes no time asking. "How was last night?"

"It was fun. We ate at *Ritzy and Spiffy*. That was my first time there, and also my first time tasting red Syrah."

"What did you have to eat?" my dad asks.

"I had a sirloin with mashed potatoes and salad. And for desert, Ben surprised me with chocolate lava cake. It was so beyond yummy!"

My parents seemed pleased.

"What else did you do?" my mom asked.

"We walked around the town pond, then came home. We didn't do anything else, Mom," I say it like that to reassure her.

"That's fine," my mom said. "Sounds like fun."

My mom and I finish eating and go back to our rooms to apply our makeup. There was a knock at the door at 8 o'clock. I love that Ben comes early. My dad is the only one available to answer the knock. This time, I'm completely ready on time and I'm waiting on Mom in the living room. Ben walks in the house, and he is wearing a striped reddish-brown, and white polo shirt with khaki pants.

"You look handsome," I offer.

He smiles and says, "Well, you look amazing!"

We hug. My dad had to watch us, which made me feel uncomfortable, so I pull away from Ben. My mom enters the room, hair and make-up in place.

"We are ready to go," I say.

"I didn't know Ben was coming too! I'm so glad." It was obvious that Mom was both surprised and pleased to know he was going with us.

We all get in my mom's car, and she drives us to church. I introduce Ben to everyone, and they all welcome him. Bible class was like it usually is. I always enjoy the discussions that happen. Of course, I don't get involved. I'd rather hide behind the book than feel embarrassed. I listen, though. I listen very carefully and think about what I am learning. I share my Bible with Ben so he can read along.

Before long, it's time for Worship. We stay in our seats as we wait for it to get quiet. There's a feeling of respect and virtue that seems ever-present. Then the song leader stands at the podium and cues us the first song. After it, Ben leans over and whispers in my ear, "You have an incredible voice."

I give him a bashful smile and mouth the word, "Thanks."

After worship, everyone is around Ben asking him questions, and getting to know him. I take it all in: watching and listening, but never saying a word. I like watching how Ben is able to handle himself. I admire it, actually. I am so shy and most times I want to hide behind a book.

Once we were outside the church, Mom brings up lunch.

"What kind of pizza do you like Ben?" she asks.

"Actually any kind except veggie," he answers.

We head over to Papa Murphy's and pick up a couple of pizzas.

When we get home, Dad greets us at the car to help with the pizzas. Mainly because he's hungry. He puts a movie in while the pizzas cook. When they are ready, we all enjoy our slices and down our pop, while glued to the TV. It was almost picturesque to me. With all of us sitting there together, it's like Ben is part of the family.

When the movie ended, Dad said, "Well, I better get back out there and finish." "What are you doing out there?" Ben asks.

"You want to come out? I will show you, but you might need to change your clothes. You don't need to get your nice clothes dirty."

My mom immediately goes into the bedroom sund gets my dad's work clothes: jeans and a stained t-shirt. Ben takes them and heads into the bathroom. He comes out messing with the jeans.

"These are a little tight, but they'll work."

I chuckle.

I can't believe he and my dad are about the same size. I also can't help but touch his chest and give him a short kiss.

"What was that for?" he said.

I shrug my shoulders and smile.

Ben hugs me, then heads out the door.

I go into my room and change into shorts. I feel like going outside and doing something.

I'm stuck in an office five days a week, I need to get some sun, so I walk outside.

Wow! I didn't realize it was this hot already. I feel like not doing anything too strenuous since it is so hot. Just a little something. Maybe I'll go find my outdoor cats and spend some time with them. I check in the shed. Nope. I walk up to the feed house. Nope. I walk back down to the house and into the shop where my dad and Ben are.

"Hey Dad, have you seen Figaro and Tiger?"

"Last time I saw them they were laying in the insulation." He points to the corner of the shop where all of the yellow insulation is neatly stacked.

Ben watches me as I walk over to the corner of the shop. I climb up on boxes and call, "Here kitty, kitty."

I hear them, but I can't see them. At least, not yet.

"Where are you, kitties? Here kitty, kitty."

Soon, Tiger appears. Then Figaro shows up. I pick them both up and walk over to Ben. "These are my outdoor kitties. They keep the mice, rabbits, and snakes away."

Ben reaches out to pes both of them. "They are so big." "They are strong too," Dad says.

"I'm going to feed them now," I say as I carry them down to the shed where their food and water are.

I fill up their food bowl, and like always, they act like they are starving. Next, I take their water dish outside and dump out their nasty stale water. I go to the hydrant next to the dog pen and wash it out and fill it up. The cold water splashing on my feet feels so good against the hot sun. I take a deep breath to take in the fresh air while I stand there, waiting for the bowl to fill up.

By this time, the kitties are outside the shed door watching me. I walk up to them and put down their water dish. My kitties follow me and take a drink. I pet them as they are lapping up the water. I hang out with them for a while longer, petting and talking to them.

After about an hour, with the kitties and the fresh air and sunshine, I go back inside to see what Mom is doing. She is sleeping on the couch, in the sun. I retreat outside and look at the shop. The radio going, and Ben and Dad are working on a truck. Now what should I do? Maybe I'll go for a walk. I decide to hike my two mile trail that I used to run when I was training for cross-country. I leave our drive way and start walking up the dirt road. Once I cross the fence on our property, I keep following what used to be the road up the hill.

Now that I'm in the grass and dirt, it's not nearly as hot. And it's also very quiet. All I hear are the grasshoppers fluttering as I walk past them, making them escape my foot and fly into the air. I'm breaking into a sweat now.

I almost make it to the top when I hear a four wheeler behind me. I turn around and see Dad driving with Ben sitting behind him.

"What are you doing?" I ask.

"We saw you leave the house. Want a ride?" Dad asks as he pats the front of the four wheeler.

Apparently he wants me to sit on top of the four wheeler in the front. "Uh, no thanks. I'll keep walking."

"Are you doing the trail?" Dad asks.

"Yes. I'll continue the loop and head home."

"Ben is staying for dinner so I'm going to go back to the house to take out the steaks."

I look at Ben. He is looking out over the horizon since we are basically on top of the hill.

Nothing really to see out here other than sagebrush and grass. I wonder what he is thinking.

"Do you want to come back with me?" Dad asks Ben.

"No. I'll finish the walk with Jess."

Ben gets off the four wheeler, and Dad turns it around and races back down the hill.

"So you have a loop, huh?" Ben asks.

"Yeah. It's two miles. I used to run it when I was training for cross-country." "How come you don't run anymore?"

That's right. He doesn't know about my knee. "I dislocated my knee a month before the season began."

"Ouch."

"Yeah. I was in therapy for the entire season, which is three long months when you're not part of the team. My coach was just as bummed as I was."

"Is that why you managed the track team instead of running and jumping?"

"Yeah. My mom doesn't want me to run anymore because if I dislocate it again then its surgery."

"Wow."

We start walking along the top of the hill now, heading towards a big dirt pit. "What is that up ahead?" Ben asks.

"My brother and I call it the antelope pit because we used to find antelope bones here." We walk down into the pit. Ben walks ahead and picks up a perfectly round rock. "This is cool. It's a rock but made out of sand, and it's perfectly round."

I smile, remembering. "I used to collect these rocks when we first moved here."

All of sudden, a loud yipping sound scares Ben and me. We turn and look back where we walked down and see a fox running into a hole on the side of the pit.

"Oh, yeah. I forgot about the fox den," I tell Ben.

"That was cool!" Ben starts running towards the den.

"I wouldn't do that if I were you," I yell to him.

Ben is right next to the den and looks inside. "It's really deep in there," he yells back at me.

I shake my head and start walking towards him. As I get closer, he whispers, "I hear something in there."

"Well, it's probably the fox we saw go in there," I say as if going "duh!"

I put my ear closer to the hole and sure enough, you could hear little yip yips. "There must be pups in there. Come on. We better leave them alone."

I grab Ben's hand and lead him away from the den. We walk out of the pit and start walking up a butte.

"Watch out for rattlesnakes," I say.

"Dude, really?" Ben says loudly, as if he's scared.

"Yeah. I used to run into them every now and then when I was out running." "What did you do?"

"Well, usually I had my dog with me, so she would let me know when there was a snake and I would just run around it, passing it."

"You are so brave," Ben says.

"No, I'm not. I'm deeply terrified of snakes. That's why I brought my dog." Ben laughs.

We make it to the top of the butte. Ben starts to sit down.

"I wouldn't do that," I say quickly before his behind touches the ground.

"Why?" Ben asks in mid squat.

"Because of the flying red ants."

"Ew!" Ben quickly stands back up.

"You are not much of an outdoors man, are you?" Ben chuckles. "I thought I was."

We look out over the vastness of the land. We can see for miles. The hills, houses, horses, grass, sagebrush, and then there's the main road.

We see the trucks and cars going here and there. We can even hear the loud semis. The sun is starting to go down in the horizon.

"You sure do know how to pick 'em," Ben says.

"Huh?" I look at him.

"The views. You know where to go to get a good view of the world." I blush.

I turn around and look back down at our house. You could also see our neighbors and their cows. Ben turns around as well.

"Your parents got a nice place."

"Yeah. It was a lot of work. When we moved here, there was a little home, a dog pen, the shed, and a water hydrant. We planted all the trees, moved the house here, built the fence, planted the yard and garden, and built the shop, barn, and corral. It took a lot of summers to get it where it is now."

We stare at the place for a while before we begin our walk down the butte. It was very steep so Ben and I helped each other down, a little bit at a time. We finally made it and walked along the fence line until we reach home.

Chapter 14

As Ben and I walk back into the house, we are greeted by my mom.

"Have a nice walk?" my mom asks.

Ben answers. "Yeah, it was great! You have a nice place here, Bev."
"Thank you!"

Then Sbabys slinks out of my room, meowing away.

"My Sbabys, my sweetness," I say in a baby voice. She comes running up to me, and I scoop her up in my arms.

"This is my sweet kitty," I show Ben.

"Hi there, sweet kitty," Ben says as he pets her.

Sbabys is not too sure of him, but tolerates it because I'm holding her. Knowing she's a little uncomfortable, I set her down. She slinks back into my bedroom.

"When is supper, Mom?" I ask.

"Whenever your dad gets done with the steaks. The potatoes and green beans are almost ready."

I look at Ben, and he looks at me. Hmmm. Not sure what to do no. We just wait? Do I show him around the house? Do I show him my room? Can't put in a movie because it's almost time to eat. Then I catch Ben peeking through the open door to my room.

"You like stars?" he asks. He sees the sun, moon, and stars border on my wall. "Yeah. There's glow-in-the-dark stars made into constellations on my ceiling." "Cool."

I think for a minute while I stand there - looking at Ben, who is looking in my room. All right. I take his hand and lead him into my room. I shut the shade, turn off the light, and close the door so it can be pitch black.

"Wow. Very cool," I hear him say.

I can't see him. It's perfectly dark. I just stand still so I don't step on him or Sbabys because I'm exactly sure where she is either. All I know is that my ceiling is lit up with stars, and there I was. Under the starts with Ben.

"What constellation is that?"

"Um, which part of the ceiling are you looking at?" I ask him this because I can't see him at all. Not even an outline of a shadow.

"The constellation next to your window."

"It's Draco."

"What about the one next to your door?"

"Um, I don't know the science term for it, but I know it's supposed to be a swan."

It's quiet for a minute that feels like an hour. I dare not move. At least I can look at the stars above. That was really all I could make out in the darkness. I feel Ben's hand touch mine. I breathe a short gasp. I am kind of startled. Now I have tingles going down my spine. His hand moves up my arm onto my shoulder. I shiver. He continues moving his hand over my shoulder across my back and down to my waist. Now I have the full on goosebumps. Where is he? Why can't I see him? Both of his hands reach for mine and I realize that he is standing behind me.

"Too bad I have to go back to work tomorrow," he whispers in my ear.

I get the tingles again. What is going on? I've never felt like this before. Then he starts swaying like as if we are dancing. His body is nice and warm. We sway to our own music, in the dark, under the stars in my bedroom.

We are interrupted by my mom who is knocking on the door. "It's time to eat."

I sigh.

We head out of the room and sit down at the table. My dad is already seated, and he notices we came out of a dark room.

"What were you two doing in there?" he says with an eyebrow raised.

"Nothing. Just looking at my glow-in-the-dark stars."

"Oh."

Nothing else was said. We say a prayer and we dig in.

Dinner tastes great and we all manage to make polite conversation. Ben, of course, is good at this. I listen a lot when he is talking to Mom and Dad. I learn more about him as he talks to my parents.

"Thank you. That was *very* good!" he says as he puts his fork and knife on his plate.

"Do we have any more cookies left?" I ask Mom.

"I think so."

I get the cookie jar and begin to pass it around. I think there is enough for all of us. "I need to make some more," I say.

"You made these?" Ben asks.

I nod my head, yes.

"They're good. Really good."

"Thanks." I blush.

"I taste a hint of tang to them," he says after a couple of bites.

"That's because I added orange flavoring."

"Really?" Ben seemed both astonished and amazed, in a very good way.

After eating two cookies, he says, "Well, I better go so I can get to bed at a decent time for work tomorrow."

I hang my head. I don't want him to go. This weekend went by so fast. And it was amazing.

"Thanks again for the food," he adds, as he gets up from the table.

He picks up his plate and silverware and places them in the sink. I do the same. I walk into my room and grab his shirt. He is waiting for me next to the sliding glass door. I hand him his shirt that will always remind me of the 4th of July.

"I washed it, but you might want to wash it again to get the cat hair off."

Ben takes it out of my hands and says, "I'm sure it will be fine. Follow me to my car?" "Sure."

I follow him to his car. We hug and give each other a gentle kiss, knowing my parents are watching from the window. I suddenly have the urge to cry. What's wrong with me? I'll see him again in a couple of weeks.

Ben gets into his car and turns the key. He looks at me through his window. I give a little wave. I think he can read my mind, and it says that I don't want him to go. He quickly opens his door and gets out of his car. He wraps his arms around me and gives me a tight hug. I squeeze him back and inhale. I make a memory of his smell. I think Ben is doing the same because I noticed his face was in my hair. I giggle and let go of him.

"I'll see you in two weeks," I say trying to hold back my tears.

"I'll call," he reassures me. He gets back into his car and drives away.

I watch, keeping my back to the window just in case my parents are still watching me. I didn't want them seeing me with tears streaming down my face. After minutes or so go by, I dry my tears away and walk back into the house.

"What are we going to watch tonight?" I ask as if nothing happened.

"You choose," my dad says.

I search for the perfect movie for all of us to enjoy. We settle in for a couple of hours of entertainment, then I head off to bed. Monday morning comes awfully early.

And…what seems like a blink of an eye, it's already Monday morning. Poo.

My entire body feels like it's dragging today. It feels like it will be forever before I get to see Ben again. I'm not sure what his hours are, so I plan on not texting or calling him. I will wait for him to call or text me when he is ready. I don't want to come on too strong. Last thing I want is for him to feel like he is suffocating. He needs space. But not too much space to where he will forget about me. *Sigh* I've been going steady with him almost two months now and I really don't want to lose this one. He is such a gentleman and quite a cutie. He even gives me the tingles at the slightest touch. There is a deep connection between us. I have never felt like this before.

After work, my phone rings. Hoping it's Ben, I quickly get my phone out of my pocket.

Instead, it's Kendra.

"Hey, Kendra! I haven't heard from you in a while. You must have service."

"Yeah, I'm in town and I was wondering what you have been doing up to this summer." "Nothing much. Just working a lot. I just got off and I'm heading home." "How's work?"

"Boring. I just do paperwork. Mindless. How about you?"

"I like my job. I'm outside all of the time. I have a nice tan, and I met some new friends." "Any of your new friends a guy?"

"No, but speaking of guys. What about that guy you gave your phone number to at state track meet?"

What am I supposed to say? I don't want to tell her about Ben, yet. "Um, well. We've been talking to each other on the phone. Even went out on a couple of dates."

"Ooooh. What's his name?"

"Um, Ben." Uh-oh. I told her. I wonder if she will suspect her coach Ben.

"What he's like?"

She doesn't suspect. *Phew!* "He's cute and a gentleman."

"Sounds like a keeper."

"He is."

It's quiet for a few seconds. I didn't know what else to say. I didn't want to tell her too much about Ben.

"Well, sounds like I better go. I still have to call my sister anyways." "Ok. You take care, Kendra. Be careful." "You too."

"Bye."

"Bye."

I hang up the phone and continue driving home. I felt relieved that I survived that call.

Chapter 15

$\mathcal{I}$ can't stand it anymore. A few days have gone by, and I haven't heard from Ben yet. I have to at least text him just in case he is still working. As soon as I get home after work on Friday afternoon I grab my phone to text him. I have to figure out what to text so I don't seem too clingy, but I want him to know that I am thinking about him. How about…How was your first week of work? I wait forever before my phone dings. Ben: Busy. A shovel went down so things got backed up.

Me: I wonder if they're going to send my dad there to help fix it.

Ben: I hope so. It needs to be fixed soon.

Me: Don't work too hard.

I didn't get a text back so he must still be working or just busy. Poor guy. It's Friday night and he can barely talk to me. I lie in bed thinking about what to do this weekend. It's the middle of July. I need to think of something to make for fair next month. I'm still in 4-H, and I still want to do the fashion revue for my last year. The last three years I took a steer to fair. That's how I got my car and some of my college money. This year, since I'm working, I couldn't do a steer, but my mom said

I could still do the fashion revue. Maybe I'll go into town tomorrow and pick out a pattern and fabric. Something easy, but still challenging enough to win a prize.

The next day, I get up early enough to get to Hancock Fabrics, in town. I find a pattern for a flowered skirt and a two-sided jacket. I choose a purple cotton fabric with silver stars on it for my skirt. I also make sure I have enough for one side of my jacket. For the other side, I chose a jean fabric. When I get home, I have enough time to cut out the patterns. Tomorrow after church, I plan on sewing.

Sewing my skirt was easy; however, my jacket is going to be my challenge. I have my mom help me. She also suggests I put a white trim along the edges so when I reverse the jacket, none of my hems will show. It will take a couple of more nights before I get my jacket done. Besides, this will help keep my mind off of Ben.

After I put my sewing stuff away for the night, my phone rings. I can see that it is Ben. "Hey!"

"Hi. Sorry I'm calling you so late."

I shrug. "It's okay. I've been keeping myself busy anyway, so that I wouldn't think about you so much. I mean … I've been thinking about you a lot. I mean …" *Oh, I'm such a dork! Stop talking before I embarrass myself some more.*

"It's alright. I've been thinking a lot about you, too. I miss you." I don't feel embarrassed anymore. "I miss you, too."

"So what have you been doing to keep yourself busy so you wouldn't think of me?"

I blush. "I'm sewing for fair."

"You sew, too?"

"Yeah. I sew whatever… and then model it for fair." "This I have to see. When are you doing this?"

I look at the calendar. "The judging is August 3rd, but I model for the public on Friday August 4th at 7."

"I will make sure I have time off to watch you."

I blush. "You don't have to. I understand if you can't make it." *Deep inside, I really wish he can make it.*

"Oh, I'm coming. Just count on it."

"K."

"When does fair start?"

I look back at my calendar. "The 28th, but the carnival isn't open 'til the 29th." "Cool, a carnival. We should go."

I smile. "We should. I would like that."

"Listen. The whole reason I'm calling is that I made arrangements." "Oh?"

"I've worked it out so I can have Saturdays and Sundays off the rest of the summer, so I can spend more time with you before you go to college. So there will be some days I have to work longer than usual."

I don't know what to say now, other than, "Wow. You did that for me? I mean…, to hang out with me?"

"Yeah. I like being with you."

I feel my face getting really red. Good thing he can't see me. "So, what does that mean for next weekend? Are you off or do you still have to work?"

"I'm off next weekend, and that's the next thing I want to ask you. Do you want to come to my house next Saturday? I'll cook."

I'm silent. The last time I got invited to a guy's house, he couldn't keep his hands off of me. This is Ben, though.

I still don't know.

"I'm inviting Jack and Liv and some other people if that makes you feel better." That does make it better. "What about Dave and Becky?" I ask.

"I'm inviting Dave too, if that's okay. But not Becky." "Yeah. That's ok. Anything you want me to bring?"

"If you want, you can bring a dessert."

"I can do that. Any type of dessert, or something specific? I can do brownies, cookies, cakes, and a pie."

"Brownies sound good."

"Brownies it is. What time on Saturday?"

"6?"

"Ok. I can't wait to see you again."

"Me too."

"Bye."

"Bye."

My mom wanders into my room, carrying the last of my sewing. "Got another date with

Ben?"

"Yeah. He has invited me over to his house on Saturday. I guess he's inviting me and the same people I met on the 4th over. Is it okay if I go?"

Mom looks at me. "Sure. Just don't be out too late." I'm so excited. I can't wait.

The week went surprisingly fast. I think it's because I've been keeping myself busy at work, and the moment I get home, I work on my jacket. I finally finish my jacket on Thursday night, so by Friday night all I could do was think about tomorrow. I plan on beautifying myself again like I did for the 4th. The difference is that I get to sleep in. That's a bonus.

Besides eating my meals, I waxed, put on a face mask, did my nails, and baked the brownies. I didn't want to do anything fancy this time, so after I showered, I chose jean shorts with a plain pink t-shirt. I'm just going to leave my hair down, but I'll straighten it. I don't want to put all my make-up on either. I just apply eye shadow, eye liner, and mascara. I do put some diamond studs in my ears though. I decide to bring a hair tie just in case I need to put my hair up.

I put the hair tie on my wrist.

Well, it's time…5:30. Time for me to go. I grab a sweatshirt and the brownies that I was cooling on the counter.

"Be back by 11," my mom yells, as I head out the door.

"I will." As I get in the car, ready to turn the key, I realize that I don't know his address.

Me: Where do u live? What's your address?

Ben: It's a little house. 325 Bighorn Ave.

Me: I'm on my way.

Ben: See you soon. ☺

I have an idea where that is and I put my car in reverse, turn on to the road, and drive off.

Chapter 16

He was right. It is a little house. I'm sure it's perfect for just him, though. I park a little further down the road, knowing other people are going to show up. I leave my sweatshirt in the car, but I take the brownies with me. I see Ben's blue car and there's another car there as well. Somebody is already here. I walk up the three steps onto a deck and knock on the door. Ben answers.

"You found it with no trouble, I see."

I nod.

I walk on in the house and wonder who else is here.

Ben takes the brownies from my hands. "Mmm. These look good."

He walks straight through a doorway into the kitchen. I follow him. He sets the brownies down on the counter, and I see a woman at the counter chopping up something. I can't really see her because her back is facing me.

"Lacey, this is Jess. Jess, this is Lacey."

Lacey stops chopping and turns around. She wipes her hands on an apron. I thought Ben was cooking. She reaches out her hand for me to shake, so I do the same. I'm wondering how Ben knows her. And I can't help but ask.

"Do you work with Ben?"

"No. I'm an old friend."

I'm not sure what that means, but I'll try to shrug it away. I see Ben head out the back sliding glass door onto the deck so I follow him. He is standing in front of a grill. Well, he is cooking. But what is she doing here? I come up behind Ben, and I can't help myself but put my hands on his back. I feel him shiver.

"Whatcha' makin'?" My hands are still on his back. I want to hug him.

"I'm making barbeque ribs."

"Yum! That sounds great."

At that moment, Lacey opens the door and pokes her head out. "Ben, can you come help me in here, please? I don't know what to do with these vegetables."

Ben sighs and heads back into the house.

I stay outside on the deck. I see that there are no chairs around, so I pull myself up on the banister so I can sit. There is a warm breeze blowing, which makes my hair go in my face every now and then. The smell of the ribs and the barbeque sauce is making my stomach rumble.

I watch what's happening in the house through the sliding glass doors. Ben puts himself next to Lacey at the counter, and both of them are cutting and sorting the vegetables. I hear a knock at the door and Ben goes to open it. Liv and Jack walk in the house. Both of them are carrying chips. I can't hear what anyone is saying, but I can see them. Liv walks into the kitchen and puts the chips on the counter, then she sees Lacey and walks over to her and they give each other a hug.

Great! Liv and Lacey know each other.

Jack and Ben are still at the door talking. I wonder what they are saying. Another knock. Since Jack is closest to the door, he opens it. Dave walks in and shuts the door behind him. Dave, Jack, and Ben are talking. It's as if they don't want the girls to listen because they keep looking towards the kitchen. I'm still sitting on the banister watching everything. Liv and Lacey act like they are best friends and haven't seen each other in a long time. They are just chatting excitedly with their hands going up and down and all over the place.

He finally sees me sitting on the banister and comes outside. "Sorry. It's chaos in there."

"It seems like it."

Ben goes back to the grill, tending to the ribs. I still stay in my spot watching everyone else. Jack and Dave go into the kitchen now. Jack pulls Liv to the side and tells something to her. Now Liv is looking at me. I wonder what's going on. I wonder if they don't want me here. I feel like an outcast.

Dave looks at Liv and Jack, and then looks in this direction, which means he's looking at me. He seems excited to see me because at that very moment, he comes outside.

He pulls himself on the banister next to me. "Been a while since I've seen you, cutie." Oh my. I scooch myself a little bit away from him. I look at Ben and he giggles. I smile

knowing what he is giggling about. Then I look back at Dave. "Yes. It has been a while. How have you been?"

"Oh, you know. I've been having to work with that guy over there. You know, all he ever talks about is you."

I look at Ben. I see his face turn red. I smile.

"I think he really likes you. Maybe even love you."

Ben walks over to Dave and pulls him down off the banister. "Alright, Dave that's enough. I think Lacey needs your help." Ben opens the sliding glass door and pushes his friend into the kitchen.

I'm giggling now. I can't help it. I try to hide my giggle behind my hand.

Ben comes back to the grill and continues putting barbeque sauce on the ribs. I come down off the banister and give him a huge hug from behind. He puts his free hand on my hands. I inhale. He always smells so good. He puts the basting brush down and closes the grill. He slowly turns around into my arms and reciprocates with even a bigger hug.

Once again, the door opens and Lacey's head pops out. "Dave doesn't know what he is doing. Can you help me please?"

Ben looks at me and gives me a peck on the lips. He once again makes his way into the house. I stay outside and I pull myself back up on the banister. I watch everyone in the house.

Ben quickly puts all the vegetables in the bowl and comes outside. He opens up the grill and starts placing corn and peppers on it. He seems agitated. Jack, Dave, and Liv all come outside with beers in their hands.

"I'm glad we could do this again," Dave says.

I get down from the banister and put my hand on Ben's back again. "Anything I can do to help?"

Ben sighs. "No. I'm fine now. I'm just glad you are here."

He finishes putting the vegetables on the grill and Lacey pokes her head out the door again. "Ben, where is your bottle opener so I can open this wine?"

Ben takes the bowl back inside the house. I stay on the deck, but I walk towards the door to get a better view of what's going on inside. I see Ben opening a top cupboard and getting a bottle opener down. Lacey takes it from his hand, and as she does, she gives him a small caress on his hand. He pulls away. I think I know what is going on now.

Dave is obviously watching me watching them because he comes behind me, startling me, and says, "I wouldn't mind Lacey too much. She likes to show up here unannounced sometimes. She lives just down the street."

"How come Ben doesn't say anything to her?" I ask.

"He has, but somehow she always has an excuse to help or needing help. Ben was interested in her at one time, but she got clingy - like calling every day while he was working or showing up at his house every time he was off. She would somehow always know when he was off or working. He finally told her to leave him alone. It didn't last long. Honestly, I would love to have a free maid."

Poor Ben. He probably got tired of finding the right girl: dating or just girls in general. I almost think that he got drugged when he slept with that one because he said he was at a party. I don't know why, but all of a sudden, I now have different feelings for Ben. It's like I can really trust him now. I have sympathy for him. I know what he feels like. I've dated four different guys just within a year. Well actually, my mom made me go out with one of them. I'm still young and have a long time yet, but Ben is three years older than me. The older he gets, the less single girls there are.

Jack speaks up over us and interrupts my thoughts and feelings. "I just want to make an announcement. Since I am here with my two closest friends, I want to say that Liv and I are getting married, and I want you two to be my groomsmen."

I smile.

Dave and Ben congratulate them both.

"When did this happen?" Dave asks.

Liv speaks up first, "He proposed to me on the 4th during the finale. It was so romantic." I turn around and see Lacey standing inside the house, right next to the door, watching everybody. She notices that I notice her and she turns around to the counter. She is a bit odd. Ben asks, "When is the wedding?"

Liv speaks up again, "We are not sure yet, but I think it will be in the spring." Then Dave asks, "How come you didn't tell us at work?"

Jack lingers then says, "Ben kept talking about Jess, so I kept it to myself."

I think my heart just dropped.

I look at Ben to see what his reaction is. He walks up to Jack and says, "I'm sorry, dude. You should've just shut me up and told us."

Jack continues, "Dude. I know what it feels like…"

I didn't hear the rest. It seems I'm kind of ruining an old relationship. I keep getting in the way, and it may be best I should just wait until my second year of college before I date again. I head inside to use the restroom. I'll go home afterwards.

I finish washing my hands and dry them on a towel. I turn the knob but the door won't open. Ok. Maybe I didn't turn the knob all the way. I turned the knob as far as it could go and push. Nothing. How come I can't get out? I start shaking the door. I grunt with frustration. What a night! First I feel like an outcast, then I'm getting in between Ben and an old friend. Now I'm stuck in his bathroom. I sit down next to the tub and start crying. I care for Ben. Ben needs his friends. My friends are finding their own way in life, and soon they won't be my friends any more. I feel alone. I don't want that for Ben.

Chapter 17

After I have a good cry, I start to dry my tears. I look at myself in the mirror and fix my hair and eyes. Then I hear a *thunk*! The knob turns and the door flies open.

"There you are!" Ben says. "Are you okay?" He hugs me.

"I'm fine now."

As I'm hugging Ben, I notice a chair sitting in the hallway, next to the door. I let go of Ben.

"Umm. Did someone put a chair up against the door?"

I look at Ben. I'm going to cry again. I don't want him to see me cry. I run past him and out the front door. I start down the stairs, but Ben grabs my hand. I have tears streaming down my face again.

"I'm sorry," Ben says. "Lacey did it. I don't know why but please stay. Have you been crying?"

He holds me close. "I'm sorry," I say through sobs. "I didn't mean to ruin your night. I didn't mean to be in your way especially coming between Jack and you. I'm sorry your friends don't like me. It's probably best I just go home." I pull away from his arms and start walking toward my car.

He grabs hold of my hand again. "Jessica, you are most definitely not in my way, and my friends like you. It's Lacey they don't like. She showed up unannounced like always. I even asked Jack and Dave to help keep her away from you and me. Then Jack asked Liv to help." He hugs me. "Jack was right about me. I couldn't stop talking about you because I'm falling in love with you. He says it happens and he understands."

Wait. What did Ben just say? Did he just tell me he is falling in love with me? I stop sniffling and crying. *Why do I keep crying?* I'm such a baby. I look at his face. He is still talking. "I honestly just wanted just the two of us, but I knew you would have been uncomfortable because you got harassed by 'octopus man'."

I laugh. "You are right, Ben. I really didn't want to come because of that, but after tonight, I now know I can trust you."

I hug him and say, "I'm falling in love with you, too."

He lets go of me and starts kissing me. We get interrupted when we hear whistling and the words, "You go, girl!" Both us smile, yet feel embarrassed. We turn and start walking back to the house, hand in hand.

Before we get to the steps, Lacey throws her apron at Ben and says, "I'm never coming back here again!" She storms off down the road.

Dave yells to her, "It's about time!"

Liv shushes him. Then we all giggle as we file into the house.

Ben gets the paper plates out and sets out the food on the counter. We take our turns getting our plates and food.

"These barbeque ribs are amazing!" I say to Ben.

"I'd like to make a toast," Dave says holding up his bottle of beer. "That we be good friends for as long as we live!"

"Here, here," Jack and Ben say.

Liv and Jack take a drink of their beer.

I smile.

It feels good to be part of a group again. I may have found my own group of friends as well. Too bad I have to go to college next month. I eat as I listen to Dave talk since he is doing most of the yakking. It seems that Jack, Dave, and Ben have been good friends for almost two years. They all got hired about the same time, so they work the same shifts.

After we get done eating, Ben brings out the brownies with a knife, so we can cut our own square.

"Guess who brought these."

Dave guesses, "Liv."

"No, Jess brought them."

They all take a bite. I watch them to see what their reactions are.

"They're good," Jack says.

"Can I have the recipe 'cause my brownies always end up hard?" Liv asks.

Ben says, "Not only do I like her, but she bakes."

I blush.

"What are we going to do now?" Liv asks.

"I have some movies, but I don't know if you girls would be interested," Ben says looking through his movie collection.

I wonder over and take a gander. "Oh. I like these movies," I say pulling *Fast and Furious* out.

"Sweet. Did I mention I like this girl, Ben?" Dave says.

"Yes, Dave. Many times."

Ben pops the movie in.

"Have any popcorn?" Liv asks.

"Yeah. Lacey put some in the cupboard. I'll go make some." I follow Ben into the kitchen.

"Do you have a cup I can borrow?" I ask.

Ben grabs a cup for me. I fill up my cup with water from the kitchen faucet.

"Do you want ice with that?" Ben asks.

"No, I'm good. Just thirsty."

Ben smiles.

I drink all the water from the cup and set it on the counter next to the sink. I turn around and lean against the counter, watching Ben take the wrapper off the popcorn bag and place it into the microwave. He pushes the 'popcorn' button and turns to look at me. He smiles and walks over to me. He places his hand under my hair and presses his lips against mine. My lips grab ahold of his lip. We exchange kisses until the microwave beeps, letting us know the popcorn is ready. We both smile and head back to the living room. We all share the popcorn and watch the movie in silence.

After the movie, Ben and I say good-bye to Jack and Liv and congratulate them again.

"I hope to see you again before you go to college," Dave says.

"I hope so, too," I say.

Then Dave looks at Ben and say, "You better keep a hold on this one, otherwise I'm going to swoop in."

"I plan on it," Ben says as he puts his arm around me.

We wave good-bye to Dave.

"Dave sure is a character," I say.

"Yeah. He's different. That's why I like him. He keeps work interesting." "I bet."

I look at the time and notice its 10:45. "Sorry, Ben, but I've also got to go." "Yeah, that's fine. You still live with your parents who watch over you."

I nod my head in agreement. "Will I see you tomorrow morning?" I ask hoping the church members didn't scare him away.

"Yes. I'll show up at your house at 8 again." I smile. I love him. Do I dare say that out loud? I won't yet. I don't want to scare him. I do, however, want a hug from him. I wander up to him and give him a big squeeze. He squeezes me back.

"I'm glad you came. I'm sorry you had a rough time in the beginning," Ben says still hugging me.

"I'm sorry I took things the wrong way and got emotional," I say back, still hugging. "Honestly," Ben lets go of me to look me in the eyes. "That tells me you don't think highly of yourself. The girls I have been with want all the attention. You don't. You seem like you want to hide. Don't hide. Shine." He kisses me. I melt. He leads me to my car and kisses me good-bye. I drive home in silence, smiling.

Chapter 18

$\mathcal{B}$en shows up promptly at 8 o'clock, like he said he would. As I put the finishing touches on my outfit, I think about Bible study and Worship, like the last time. After church, we will grab some pizza at Papa Murphy's. I ask Mom if we can go to the grocery store to pick up some groceries because I plan on making stuffed mushrooms tonight. I want to surprise Ben with it, as well as homemade spaghetti, French bread, and a salad. I quickly grab what I need, knowing everyone's hungry for lunch. We head home and bake the pizzas. Dad slips in a movie again while we wait. After the pizzas are done, we eat and watch the movie.

Around 2 o'clock, I tell Mom that I'm planning on making supper tonight to return the favor from the night before.

"Want to walk the loop again?" I ask Ben.

"Sure."

We go outside and walk together, hand in hand. Today was not as hot as usual. It was just warm, but I know I could still work up a sweat if I did something to exert myself. By the time we reach the fence, I'm breaking a sweat. The grasshoppers and flies are all around as we walk through the grass on the beaten trail. It used to be a road. With supper on my mind, I bring up the topic of food. I'm interested to know what kinds of food Ben likes. He says he likes almost anything. Sounds like a typical guy.

"What kind of foods do you *not* like?" I ask.

"I'm not much for sour foods like pineapple, green apples, lemons, and limes." I make a note of that in my mind.

"What about you?" he asks.

"Well, you know I don't like mushrooms. And gravy, and nuts."

"I'll try to remember that," Ben says.

We continue our walk, talking about random things, getting to know each other more. We finish our walk and Dad calls from the shop.

"Tell him I'm going to make supper," I say.

"What are you making?" Ben asks.

"Spaghetti with bread, salad, and a surprise."

"Sounds good."

Ben walks up to the shop, and I walk back in the house. I start making the spaghetti sauce first since it takes about an hour to simmer. Then I start making the stuffed mushrooms and boil the noodles. I make the salad while the mushrooms bake. By now, Dad and Ben walk in the house. I look at Ben.

"Oh, no. You got your nice shirt dirty."

"It will wash. I don't think it will stain," Dad says.

"Yeah, it will be fine," Ben agrees.

"Smells good," Dad says.

"I wonder what the surprise is," Ben says as he sits at the table.

I smirk.

I work around Ben as I set the table. I place the noodles, spaghetti sauce, and salad on various places on the table. Last but not least, I pull the pan of mushrooms out of the oven and set it on the table.

"Wow. You made stuffed mushrooms." Ben seems impressed. "Can I?" he asks. His hand is in mid-air, aiming for the mushrooms.

I nod my head.

He takes one and pops the whole thing in his mouth. "These are tasty!" He grabs another and also pops it in his mouth. Then we all sit at the table and say a prayer. My mom cuts the French bread and hands it out to us. We pass the rest of the food around.

After we eat, Ben puts his hand on my shoulder and says, "That was amazing."

In that minute, I realize I have no more cookies. I've been busy sewing instead of baking. "I don't have any more cookies. Sorry."

"Oh," Ben says as he gets up from his chair. He heads out the door.

I look at my family, and my family looks at me.

I shrug and shake my head as if saying, "I don't know." Ben comes back in with my pan of brownies.

"Oh, yeah. I forgot that yesterday," I said.

"And there are some left," Ben says as he sits it down on the table and sits back down. We all dig in. After all the brownies are gone, I start picking up the dishes and putting the food away. Ben helps. The rest of my family watches a movie. When I start washing the pans and dishes, he comes up behind me.

"Want help?" Ben asks.

"Sure. You can dry." I hand him a towel.

As we stand side by side with our hips touching, we get into a rhythm. I'm washing and rinsing the dishes and handing them to Ben. Ben dries them with a towel and sets them down on the counter. I really feel like a couple now. We're doing things together, and I know him so much better than I did a month ago. Are we officially boyfriend/girlfriend? I believe we are, but does he feel the same about me as I do about him? We finish with the dishes and I put them away.

"Thanks for your help," I tell him.

I can't help it. I need to give him a hug. I love hugging him.

He returns the hug. "You're welcome."

We stand in the kitchen a little longer, hugging and swaying, as if we are dancing to our own music again.

"I better go," he says. "That alarm clock is rude to me in the early morning." I laugh.

I walk him out to his car and we exchange kisses again.

"I'll see you next weekend," he says.

I nod my head and watch him drive away before I head back in.

I find a spot on the couch and finish watching the movie with my family.

As I'm scanning papers at work the next day, I think of plans for Saturday because that is when the fair starts. I don't think there is anything special going on that day. I do, however, have to hand in my skirt and jacket then because the judging is next Monday the 31st. That reminds me, I have to hand in my two weeks' notice and take a day off. I can't believe I have two weeks left of work. Then it's state fair, and then I am going to college. I don't have much time left with Ben.

After I do my scanning, I go up to the HR department, hand in my notice, and ask for next Thursday off. By the time I'm done, it's lunch time. I go back downstairs to clock out and back to my desk to eat lunch. My thoughts go back to Ben and plans for Saturday. I'm not sure when the carnival starts so as I'm eating my sandwich, I search the Internet for the county fair. I see that the carnival starts at one. I'm thinking we could go out to eat for lunch, then head to the carnival. So far, that's all I come up with on Saturday. Maybe Ben will have some other ideas on what to do, or we will just wing it. I'll text him the plans I have so far as soon as I get off work. At 5 o'clock, I clock out and head out for my car. Before I get in, I start texting him. Let me know what you think of these plans. I was thinking of eating lunch here in town, then we would go to the carnival. The carnival doesn't open until 1. He can read it and text me back on his own time. I know he's busy. Once I am in my car, I blast my AC. It's so hot outside. I drive on home as my car cools down.

After supper and a nice hot shower, my phone dings. I open it and it read: Sounds great!

How about we eat lunch there at the carnival, then we eat supper at a restaurant?

Me: That sounds even better!

Ben: K. I'll pick u up at your house around 11. I have to do some things around here before I go anywhere.

Me: Sounds great to me. Can't wait.

Ben: Me too. Xoxo

Aww. He sent me hugs and kisses through the phone. I reply Xoxo.

I close my phone and put it on my nightstand. As I lie in bed, I still wonder, is he my boyfriend? If I introduce him to someone, what do I say? "Hi, this is my boyfriend Ben. Hi, this is Ben. I'm going out with him. Hi, this is just Ben." I end up falling asleep thinking about him.

The rest of the week goes normally, and it's finally Saturday morning. Ben and I haven't talked since Monday night. I lie in bed and wonder what Ben had to do this morning before he could see me. He might be doing housework like laundry and cleaning. I understand that. He owns a house, and he has to maintain it and take care of it himself. I stay in bed longer than usual, petting Sbabys and thinking.

By 8:30, I finally slide out of bed. I put on a tank top and jean shorts. I put my hair up in a ponytail and put my eye make-up on. I probably should wax my eyebrows today, but that's all I'll do today. I'm not going to beautify myself like I have been the other times I have seen Ben. Instead, I'll take care of my kitties and enjoy the morning to myself. It wasn't long until the clock said 10:45. Not sure what I want to do now. I don't want to put in a movie since I'll be leaving soon. I start cleaning my room. My room is generally clean, but I dust my dressers and vacuum. I sort my dirty clothes. Maybe I'll wash them later.

I organize my closet.

I'm done. I look at the clock. It's 11:15. Huh. He's late. Normally, he's usually early. I check my phone just in case he texted me while I was busy. Nothing. I sit in the rocking chair and wait. I don't want to be clingy, but I'm getting worried. It's 11:30 now. Now I'm worried and I can't help myself.

I text him. Are you on your way?

I wait.

My phone dings. Look outside.

I get up from the chair and I look out the window. I see his car, but where is he? I look out the door. I see Dad and Ben up at the shop just standing, looking at the house, talking. I wonder how long he's been here. I slip my sandals on and walk up to the shop.

"Sorry. I called Ben up here when he showed up," Dad said.

"That's fine. I was just wondering where he was," I say blushing. I hope I don't seem too clingy. I was just worried.

"Are you ready to go?" Ben asks.

"Yeah. Just let me grab my skirt and jacket."

I run back to the house, and into my room, grab my outfit, and run back outside. Ben is waiting for me next to his car. He helps me in and waves at my dad. Dad waves back. Ben crawls in the car, and we drive away.

"Sorry I was a little late," Ben says when we get on the main road.

"I don't know when you showed up," I said. "When 11:30 came, I got worried and texted you. You normally show up early for everything. Sorry."

"Don't say sorry," Ben says as he takes ahold of my hand. "I'm trying to say sorry for being late. I had to finish my laundry."

I smile knowing I guessed right on what he was doing this morning. On the rest of the drive, we listen and sing to the music on the radio.

We make it to the fair grounds. It's so hot already. The heat just blasts me as I get out of the car. I look around remembering what it was like bringing my steers here. I see families unloading their animals and pushing and pulling them into their cages or stalls.

"I've never been here before. Where do we find food?" Ben asks.

I take hold of his hand and say, "This way."

I lead him inside the first barn where the pigs are. It's already smelly.

"Wow. It's full of pigs in here. And stinky," Ben says covering his nose.

"Yeah. Pigs are usually stinky. That's why I did steers," I say leading Ben through the maze of gates.

"You brought a steer to fair?" Ben asks in amazement.

I nod my head, yes.

"You surprise me every time I see you," Ben says.

We make it out of the pig barn and into the concession area. Ben gets us each a hot dog and a plate of nachos to share.

Chapter 19

$\mathcal{W}$e go outside under a tent to eat. I look at the board for the entertainment hours.

"In about a half hour, the hypnotist is going to be on," I tell Ben.

"That will be interesting to see. Do you believe he can do it?"

I look at him. "Yes. He hypnotizes me a couple of times a year," I answer, being a little harsh in my tone.

Ben looks at me in amazement again. "You've done this before? Were you really under? What did it feel like? Do you remember anything?"

I smile. Then I tell him, "No. I don't remember anything. It just feels like I took a good nap. I have to ask people what he made do."

Ben looks at the stage for a moment, then says, "I wonder what he will make me do." Now I'm surprised. "Are you planning to do it?" I ask. "Only if you do it with me," Ben says taking my hand.

"Aww, but then I won't be able to tell you what he made you do. I want to watch you get hypnotized," I say, trying to be cute.

"No. You're doing it with me," he says squeezing my hand.

Ok. I'll be there to support him. I wish somebody I knew was here so they can video record us. The show starts how it begins every year. The hypnotist messes with our minds with a spinning black and white spiral fan. Then he asks for volunteers. Ben and I raise our hands with a couple of other people. He chooses us and we walk up on stage, hand in hand.

"Are you two a couple?" he asks Ben and me. I don't know how to answer that, so I let Ben answer. Ben nods his head yes.

The hypnotist looks at the audience and says, "This is going to be fun."

The audience laughs.

Ben seems nervous. I can tell because he is squeezing my hand so tightly.

"I will have to split you up though," the hypnotist says.

He sits Ben down on a chair on the far end of the stage. Then he puts me between two guys. I forgot that's how he sets up his stage. He always arranges his subjects boy, girl, boy, girl. Within minutes, the hypnotist fills up his chairs and starts putting us to sleep. The last thing I remember is seeing a blue sky behind a blue ocean.

The next thing I know, I wake up to a snap! "You may go back to your seats," the hypnotist says.

Are we done already? I want to sleep more. I go to sit at the table where Ben and I were eating. I'm feeling like a zombie. Then Ben sits down next to me. We don't acknowledge each other, and he is acting like a zombie, too. The hypnotist is talking but I'm not really listening.

Then I hear a key word and I stand up and start singing "Twinkle Twinkle Little Star" like a baby. I finish and sit down. I feel embarrassed. I try to make myself small. I'm wide awake now. I look at Ben. He's still acting like a zombie. I don't dare touch him. I might scare him. The hypnotist says some more key words and random people from the audience are doing what he told them to do. Ben hasn't done anything yet. The hypnotist keeps talking and says another keyword.

Ben gets up and shouts, "Mary Jane! Mary Jane!"

Then another girl from the audience shouts, "Here Spiderman. Save me!" The audience is laughing now.

Ben runs to her and picks her up. Both Ben and the unfamiliar girl are looking at each other. Then Ben drops her back down, walks back hunched over, and sits down next to me. He

puts his arm around me and his face is beet red. I look at "Mary Jane" and she's staring at Ben.

The audience is still laughing. I'm kind of laughing myself.

Ben whispers in my ear, "What just happened? Why was I holding that girl?" I whisper back to Ben, "You were Spiderman. My hero."

Ben blushes.

"That's all for today," the hypnotist says. Then he starts advertising his CDs and DVDs. I look at the time on my phone. It's 2 o'clock. I glance at Ben, who seems to still be embarrassed by what just happened. He's staring at the grass or his feet. I can't really tell.

"Are you okay?" I ask.

Ben doesn't say a word.

"Do you feel okay? Some people get sick afterwards. Do I need to bring a garbage can over?" I ask knowing what we had for lunch. I start getting up from the picnic table to get a trash can.

Ben finally says, "I'm okay. I'm not sick."

I sit back down and rub Ben's back. "Are you okay?" I ask again.

He looks at me. "Do you remember anything?" He seems worried.

"I don't. I never do," I tell him.

Ben looks back at the grass. "I might have been dreaming this, but we were making out." I shrug and say, "We've kissed before. Nothing really new."

Ben looks at me and says it again, "We were making out, like I was feeling you."

My eyes grew big. I stop rubbing Ben's back. I look at the grass now, and I'm thinking out loud, "You don't suppose we did that in front of everyone. Did we?"

Ben shrugs. "I hope not. I hope I was just dreaming."

Then an older lady walks up to us and says, "You guys make a cute couple. You've got a keeper there." She nudges me.

"Thanks," I say.

I look at Ben. "Maybe you were just dreaming."

Then two young men walks up to us. One of them says, "If I had a hot girl like that, I would get it on too."

Ben didn't make a reaction or move, so the young men walk away. I heard one say, "What's his problem?"

I look at Ben again. He seems troubled. I rub his back again. I don't know what to say because I don't know what happened. Maybe I need to ask some people what they saw. There are a couple of people left under the tent with us. I'll ask them, just so I know what we did on stage in front of everyone. I leave Ben at the picnic table as I walk up to a woman a little older than me.

"I'm sorry. May I ask what the hypnotist make my boy...?" I almost said it. I almost said boyfriend. I don't think Ben can hear. I'll go ahead and say it. "What did the hypnotist make my boyfriend and I do? Just the two of us together. You don't have to tell me the whole show."

The lady looks at me in bewilderment. "You don't remember?"

It seems like I'm the only one who gets hypnotized that doesn't remember.

She leans in closer to me. "You and another guy kissed. It was just a peck. Then, the guy you kissed started putting his hand on you." She puts her own hand on her breast, showing me where the guy was going to touch me.

"Your boyfriend pulled him away. Then he started hugging and kissing you." That's not so bad. Or she's making it sound not so bad. I better ask a more specific question.

"Was my boyfriend touching me like...?" I mimic her, putting my own hand on my breast.

The lady shakes her head no.

I nod my head. "Thanks," I said and walked back to Ben.

Ben was still hanging his head.

"You didn't do anything to me, Ben. You're fine." "I heard," he said.

I blush. He heard everything, which means he heard me call him my boyfriend.

Then why did he seem so down? "What's wrong?" I ask.

"You just can't get away from creeps, can you?"

I slump and shake my head no. Then I say, "It's okay, though. I have lived with it since puberty. Most guys stop when I tell them to. I've never really had to fight except with 'octopus man'. He couldn't get far 'cause I wouldn't let him. Besides, I took karate classes with my brother and Mom." I do some punches in the air. I'm trying to make Ben feel better so we can go on the rides.

Ben looks at me and smiles, "Did you really take karate classes, or are just saying that to make me feel better?"

"I really did take karate classes, and yes, I'm trying to make you feel better," I say, being honest.

He smiles, "I liked it when you called me your boyfriend."

I blush and say, "I hope that's okay."

"It's more than okay," he says. "It's perfect."

"Well, should we go ride some rides?" I ask. I can't hide my excitement.

"Yes, we should."

Ben takes hold of my hand and helps me up from the picnic table. We walk over to the carnival. He buys us two wrist bands. We wander around a bit, looking for the most fun rides to do. We found out that we both like the same kind of rides! As we were walking through the midway, we came upon a game that looked pretty easy. This particular one is where you have to pop balloons by throwing darts at them. I take a long hard look at it. Then my eyes turn to a big stuffed gray, kitty with long whiskers and a pink nose. It was hanging right above the balloons, and it was adorable! Ben noticed I was looking at it because he asked if he should try to win it for me.

"You don't have to, Ben. You've spent enough money as it is," I say as he walks over to the game.

"But I'm here to have fun, and I'm going to win this kitty for you."

He's persistent. He hands over the money to the guy and gets five darts to pop five balloons. Ben is pretty good! He got four out of five! But it wasn't good enough to get the kitty. So he hands over more money.

"I better get it this time. Otherwise, I have to go visit the ATM," he mumbles… more to himself.

I keep silent, watching him.

He got three so far. The third one was a lucky shot. I'm surprised the balloon popped.

The fourth one is good.

I hold my breath when he throws the fifth.

Right smack in the middle of the balloon! I shriek with excitement.

"Okay. Which one for the lady?" the guy behind the counter asks.

Ben points and says, "The gray kitty."

He takes the kitty down and automatically hands it to me. I hug the kitty. It's surprisingly soft and clean for being outside all day. Ben puts his arm around me.

"Thank you," I say and kiss him.

"You're welcome," Ben replies.

I don't think I've ever seen a bigger smile than what's on Ben's face right now. He seems so proud.

"I don't trust anyone to hold the kitty for us, so let's give the kitty a ride on the Ferris wheel," Ben suggests.

I smile, hug the kitty, and say, "I agree."

We stand in line, waiting to get on.

"Jessica Brown? What are you doing here?"

I turn around and see Sarah. "I'm uh…"

"Where did you get that kitty? Did you win it? He's cute." I look at Ben, and he's blushing.

Sarah continues, "He is cute. Who is he?"

Now I know how to introduce him. "He's my boyfriend, Ben. Ben, this is Sarah. I went to school with her, and I bet she has all sorts of animals here at the fair."

Sarah smiles. "I do. I brought 3 goats, a steer, 3 bunnies, and 2 pigs." Sarah seemed real proud of herself - as usual.

I smile.

"Wait," Sarah realizes something. "Is this the Ben that coaches Kendra? The pole vaulting coach?"

My face makes an expression that says, "Uh-oh." I look at Ben. Ben has the same expression.

Sarah gets the idea and says, "Don't worry. Your secret is safe with me."

Ben is now holding the gate for me to get on the Ferris wheel. "I better go. I'll talk to you when I come back down," I tell Sarah.

I go through the gate, and Ben helps me into the bucket. I'm holding onto the kitty as tight as I can. I'm not great with heights, but as long as I don't look down, I'll be okay. The Ferris wheel takes us around and up, up.

"Another great view," Ben says.

I look in the direction he is looking, out toward the train tracks and fields. Everything feels perfect. I sigh. Ben looks at me and pushes a stray hair out of my face. He has such gorgeous eyes. The sun is shining right in them, leaving the white dot in the blue like you see in anime cartoons. I feel all warm inside and I know it's not just from the sun. Ben lays his hand on my leg and scooches closer to me. I have tingles going from where he is touching me to my spine. He leans in closer and kisses me. We exchange kisses once more. I'm holding on to the kitty with a firm grip, while Ben puts his other hand on the back of my neck.

"Whoo! Those two are really going at it!"

Ben stops and we both look up. We see another couple above us, looking, watching us.

We wave at them, and they wave back.

I lay my head on his shoulder. Mostly to smell him again. The Ferris wheel starts moving to the top. I keep my head down so I'm not looking out and over the bucket. We round the top and start coming back down. The Ferris wheel stops again. I didn't realize Ben's arm was behind me until we stop because then his hand ends up on my shoulder. I look at him, and he is looking down over the bucket. I don't want to look where he's looking. Instead, I hug my kitty.

"They're letting people off," he says.

I look straight forward and I see the rides going around and side by side. Some of the lights are starting to turn on. The Ferris wheel moves again. I see now that we have to stop and go two more times before we get off.

"Are you having fun?" Ben asks me.

"Yes, I am. I'm glad we got to do this today."

I take the phone out of my pocket to look at the time. It's 5 o'clock. "Ben. I have to hand in my skirt and jacket as soon as we get off." He smiles. "Okay."

Finally, it's our turn. Ben helps me out of the bucket, and we walk hand in hand back to his car. This time we walk around the pig barn to get back. I tell Ben to drive around to the other building since that's where the exhibits are. He maneuvers his car to the other building across the way.

"Stay here. I'll be right back," I say to Ben.

I grab my jacket and skirt and run inside. I put my name on two cards, and lay the cards on my outfit. I run back outside to Ben.

"Where do you want to eat?" he asks.

"Honestly, as long as it's not Mexican, I don't care." Ben thinks for a moment, then says, "I know a place." We drive off.

Chapter 20

$\mathcal{W}$e pull into Applebee's.

"I haven't eaten here in a long time. I think the last time I ate at an Applebee's was with the track team," I tell Ben.

"I wasn't with you guys then." It seems he's trying to remember.

"Yeah, I don't think you were with us. You rarely came with us to out-of-town track meets."

"I mostly had to work."

The hostess sits us down at a booth and hands each of us a menu. We both order our drinks, then start looking through our choices for food.

"You want to do the 2 for $20 deal?" Ben asks.

"Sure."

"What would you like for an appetizer?" he asks.

I look. "I like anything except the chips and artichoke dip." "K."

Then we look at the entrees. I'm going to get the oriental chicken salad. It looks delicious. I close the menu.

"Already know what you want, huh?" Ben asks, still looking at the menu.

"Yep," and I take a sip of my water.

Ben then closes his menu and drinks his Mountain Dew. It seems the waitress was watching us because she immediately comes over to take our order. Once she leaves, Ben and I look at each other, like we're waiting for one of us to say something.

And then it came out like this:

"When do you…"

"I was wondering…"

Both of us were speaking at the same time.

"You first," I tell Ben.

"No. Ladies first," then he takes a drink.

I sigh. "I was wondering if you wanted to go back to the fair next Saturday because they have a free barbeque going on for the public. Plus, I wouldn't mind looking at the exhibits."

"Yeah. We can do that. I like food that's free," Ben says with a smile.

I smile then say, "What was it that you were going to say?"

"Oh, yeah." Ben puts his glass down. "I was wondering when you leave for college." I hang my head. I didn't want to think about that yet. Summer is going by faster than I want it to. "We can start moving into our dorms the weekend of the 26th. New student orientation is the same day. My classes start the 28th."

Ben nods his head. "That's sooner than I expected."

"Yeah. It's not that far away. I handed in my two week notice just this last Monday." "How can you hand in your two week notice when you have like four weeks left?" He realizes he's talking loudly and calms himself back down. "You're not planning on leaving sooner, are you?"

I shake my head. "No. The last two weeks I have off because of state fair and a week for me to pack. I'm not saying I'll win at fair, but just in case."

Ben nods his head up and down. He understands now. Then he asks, "If you do win, are you gone a whole week?"

I nod my head, yes. "If I get in the top 10, I have to show up to Douglas by the 12th. I come home on the 19th."

"What do you do there for a whole week?"

"I hang out and model, again."

Ben nods his head again. "Do you have to ride with the 4-H group down, or do you drive yourself?"

"My mom usually takes me, but that's because she usually helps with chaperoning. I don't think she's going to do that this year."

"Can I drive you down? That is, if you win."

I smile and nod my head yes. "I may not get in the top 10 this year though, so don't plan on it."

"Why you say that?"

"The other two years I've done it, I made something challenging. This year I didn't because I had to work every day."

"And don't forget you had me bugging you," Ben says, as he hangs his head.

I slide my hand across the table and take his hand. I make sure he is looking at my face when I'm talking. "You are the best thing that happened to me this summer. I would've been really bored if it wasn't for you."

He squeezes my hand.

We look at each for a while, then our food shows up. We let go of each other's hand so the waitress has more room for our food. Once we are done, Ben pays the waitress and we get up to go.

We walk out of the restaurant and the sun is barely peeking over the town. We both take a moment to admire it. It glows in the sky with blues, pinks, oranges, and yellows in the sky.

Ben inhales and says, "With you, I stop and notice the beauty of this Earth. I never used to do that."

I look at him, and say, "And to think, God made it all for us to enjoy. Including you. He definitely didn't break the mold with you."

Ben looks at me and kisses my forehead. He puts his arm around me, and we walk to the car.

As we drive to my house, Ben reaches over to hold my hand. When we get there, I let myself out of the car. Ben meets me half way. We start hugging and kissing. It's like Ben was holding his emotions all the way here and couldn't help himself but love me. I couldn't help myself but enjoy it and return it.

Ben finally releases me and says, "I'll see you tomorrow morn." I lick my lips and nod my head.

He gets back in his car and drives away. I stand in the driveway.

What just happened? I feel like I'm part of a movie now and my prince just bid me a farewell. I'm all warm and tingly inside. I try to shake it away. Now, I'm getting goosebumps. I know it's not the air because it's rather hot. I think my body is finally reacting to the kissing we just did. I rub my arms and walk in the house.

"You're home early," my mom says as I walk in. "Yeah. We just did the carnival and ate at Applebee's." "Is Ben coming over again tomorrow?" Dad asks. "I believe so," I say walking into my room.

I still have the goosebumps and feel flushed, and I didn't want my parents to see. Maybe if I take a shower, they will go away. I take off my clothes and hop in the shower. I make the water extra hot. I'm feeling better now. I rub my arms again to check if they are still there. I start remembering the kissing we did. His hands has a hold of the back of my shirt, squeezing me tighter against him. His kisses were wild and he was adding tongue. My hands were on his head, messing up his hair. It was like a movie moment.

I shiver again in the hot shower, and I realize I'm hugging myself. I got to focus: get clean and get out. I finish my shower and dry myself off. I look at myself in the mirror. I have a towel on my head. I start dreaming again. This time, it's like I'm watching Ben kissing me in slow motion. I shake my head and my towel falls from it. I have to stop day dreaming. I hug myself again, feeling cold from my wet hair.

It felt so good to be so close to Ben like that. Our bodies holding on to each other, mingling. I shake my head again and decide to get my jammies on. Then I crawl into bed. I look at my alarm clock and it reads 8:36. I look at my ceiling and start thinking about Ben. This time I'm thinking about what he might have been feeling during this new make-out session we just had. I roll to my side and stare out my window. Some stars are peeking out from the sky and I see the moonlight. The bush in front of my window is swaying in the wind. I wonder what he's thinking right now, and I fall asleep.

The next day, we do our normal church and pizza routine. After pizza and the movie, my dad asks Ben for some help in the garage. (That's why Dad asked if Ben was coming over.) This time, Ben came prepared and brought his own work clothes. He changes in the bathroom and leaves the house. Instead of going outside in the heat, I decide to play the piano. I play all the songs I know, including some church hymns.

A dirty Ben and Dad finally come back into the house. By now it's like 4 o'clock. They both go in separate bathrooms to wash their hands. Ben sees me at the piano and sits next to me on the bench.

"Can I hear you play?" he asks.

"Sure."

Since I have the hymnal book out, I flip through the pages to find one I especially like to play. I choose "God is So Good". I start playing. Thank goodness Ben is still because I was nervous at first. However, after the first verse, I begin to relax.

I only played three verses and ended it.

"That was good," he says and hugs me with one arm. Then he asks, "I was wondering if you wanted to watch a movie with me tonight."

"Sure. Just let me change out of my skirt," I say as I close the piano.

I get up from the bench and head to my room. I take off my skirt and put on some shorts. I come out of my room and see that the bathroom door is shut. He must be in there. After I sit down at the table, he walks out, and he is back in his church clothes. I stand up and offer my hand. He takes it, and we walk out to his car. We buckle in.

Before he starts the car, he asks, "Want to get a bite to eat before the movie?" I smile. "That sounds good."

We get into town and stop at *Good Times*, a burger and taco restaurant. We walk in and order our food. We sit down at a high table with high stools. Ben holds my hand from across the table. Both of us are silent for a moment. The place is pretty quiet in general. The only sounds we hear are the TVs, and they are muffled. The workers themselves are pretty quiet. I look around and see an older couple sitting in a booth next to the window, eating quietly. Then Ben speaks up.

"So, you want to be a music teacher?"

I nod my head yes.

"I think you will be good. You sing and play well." "Thanks," I say without blushing.

I must be getting used to his compliments, or just getting used to him.

Our food comes to our table. While we eat, we watch the TVs that are hanging from the ceiling. When we are ready to leave, I use the restroom to freshen up. Ben is waiting for me next to the door as I come out.

"Ready for a movie?" he asks as he offers his arm.

I smile, nod, and take his arm.

When we arrive at the movie theater, we ended up walking in with a bunch of other people. Compared to *Good Times*, this place is noisy; everyone's talking so that I can't really hear one conversation. There are so many people. Both Ben and I are looking at the board to see what is playing. *Pirates of the Caribbean: Dead Man's Chest* is playing soon. That must be why all the people are here.

"Want to see *Pirates of the Caribbean*?" Ben asks.

"Sounds good to me," I say.

We wait in line for a-while before we finally get up to the counter, and Ben buys the tickets, two drinks, and a large popcorn. We head to our theater and find a spot. The theater is quite full already, so we have to choose where ever two side by side seats are available. Ben and I share the popcorn the moment we sit down. When it runs out, he puts his arm around me. There it stayed until the movie was over.

We walk out of the theater and it's practically dark.

"My goodness it's late," Ben says. "I need to get home and sleep."

I nod my head, understanding that Ben has to get up early in the morning for work.

On the way home, I'm wondering if Ben is going to be able to get off work early enough to see me model Friday night. I don't really want to ask because I don't want to be pushy, but then I really want to know.

"Something on your mind?" Ben must've noticed I was thinking hard.

I might as well ask now. "I was wondering if I was going to see you Friday night." "What's going on Friday night?"

He must have forgotten. "I'm modeling. At 7 o'clock." "That's this week already?!" Ben exclaims.

"Yes. It's this week already. I'm modeling in front of the judges Thursday morning. I'm a bit nervous."

"Don't be nervous," he says, squeezing my hand. "I'm sure you will do great. You are already pretty."

I scoff. "It's not if I'm pretty or not. It's about how I model the outfit I'm wearing. I need to practice this week."

Ben nods his head. I think he understands what I'm saying. He says again, "You'll be fine. I'll be there for you Friday night."

I smile at him. I'm glad he's going to try to make it.

Within minutes, we arrived at my house. I get out of the car myself. We meet in front of his car again. This time we hug. We are just holding each other, taking each other in. I inhale deeply, then let go of him. I kiss him. Normally, Ben has been in control of the kissing. I feel I have had enough experience, thanks to Ben, of kissing and I take control.

I stop to look at him. I lick my lips, still tasting his. Ben still had his eyes shut. He finally exhales. I stare at him, waiting for him to say something or move.

"Ben?"

"I...I...I can't feel my legs," he mutters.

I look at the ground and giggle. "Need help to your car," I offer.

"Please."

I giggle again and take his arm. I put his arm around my neck, and I put my arm around his waist. I walk him back to the driver's side of the car. I open his car door and sit him down.

As I grab the car door to shut it, Ben says, "Wait!"

Now he is back out of the car. He takes hold of my face. Once again, he starts kissing me like yesterday. This time, I take in every second, every moment. I shiver and goosebumps show up on my skin again.

Ben stops.

He rubs my arms. I think he feels my goosebumps.

"I'm sorry," he says.

I still feel weak from the kissing. I open my eyes.

"For what?" I ask.

"I just want to be with you. The way you make me feel. I can't help myself." I remind him, "As long this is all we are doing."

Ben nods his head and looks at his car.

I say, "Yeah, I know. You got to go."

Ben looks back at me and smiles. He kisses me again and gets back in his car. I watch him drive away once more.

Chapter 21

This week is going to be short for me. The moment I get home from work, I practice my modeling. I somehow have to show that my jacket is reversible. Since my jacket and skirt are at the fair on display, I use another jacket and pretend it is changeable. My first attempt, I took my jacket off and reversed it. It was too much. Then I thought maybe I can open the jacket and show the inside of it while I wear it. Which side should I wear out? I practice different ways. When I find the right motions and gestures, I show it to my mom. She says I should wear the fabric that matches my skirt out first, then show the jean side.

Thursday morning I wake up as usual. I put on a pair of jeans and a pink undershirt with a see-through white tank top. I plan to wear the tops under my jacket. I pull my hair half way up and add some curls. Then I carefully apply my Mary Kay make-up. I want to look my best. I don't want to wear too much jewelry, so I put in purple flowers for earrings and a purple and silver choker. Next, I put on my white high-heeled sandals.

My mom drives me in for my judging. The first place I need to go is the exhibit hall to pick up my outfit. Then she drives me to the school where the judging is taking place. I look for my name on the list. I don't model until 10:15. I have about an hour to wait before it's my turn. While I wait, I mingle. I talk to some of the girls that I have done fashion revue with before. It makes the time go faster. At 10 o'clock, I wait in line against the wall with the other girls who are waiting their turn in the classroom with the judges.

My phone dings in my purse. I know its Ben. I open the phone and it read: Have u modeled yet? How did u do?

Me: I haven't modeled yet. I'm waiting in line for my turn. I won't know how I did until tomorrow night.

Ben: Sorry. Good luck!

Me: Thanks. Xoxo

The girl in front of me walks into the classroom and shuts the door. I'm next and I'm nervous. I shake my head and remind myself I can't get nervous. If I get nervous, then I'll mess up.

Don't get nervous, don't get nervous, don't get nervous.

The door opens and the girl before me walks out. My turn.

I exhale and walk in.

First impressions are important, so I make sure I am smiling as I walk in. I start modeling. The first turn is perfect as my skirt flowers out. I walk to my second turn and do a half turn so they can see the back side of me. Then I walk to my final turn. I spin and show my jacket's reverse side. I stand and wait for them to say it's okay to walk up to their table. One of the ladies singles me with her hand. I walk to the table. The judges ask me questions like my name, how old I am, and how long it took me to make the outfit. One of the ladies ask me to take off the jacket so she can have a closer look. She hands it back to me and tells me to send in the next lady. I also have to make a last impression so they can remember me, so in a very professional manner, I walk to the door. Then I turn my head and flash a smile. They are all smiling back at me. That's a good sign. I open the door to the let the next lady in.

I exhale. I did it. Now I have my public revue to do tomorrow night. I'm more nervous about that one because everyone is going to watch me, including Ben.

My mom drives me home, and I get to enjoy the rest of the day to myself. I take off my outfit and put on comfortable clothes. I wash the skirt and jacket to get ready for tomorrow, then I put in a movie. Sbabys is in my lap. She sure is enjoying me being home. I like it when she snuggles with me.

During the movie, my phone dings. I open it.

Ben: How do u think you did?

Me: I think I did ok.

Ben: I bet u did good and u get to go to state.

Me: We'll see. Aren't u supposed to be working?

Ben: Taking a break. What time should I be there tomorrow?

Me: Idk when I will be modeling, but it starts at 7. I can't wait to see u afterwards.

Ben: Can Dave, Jack and Liv come too? I told Dave and Jack about it.

Me: Sure.

Great! More reasons for me to be nervous.

Ben: Gotta get back to work. See ya. xoxo

Me: See you tomorrow. Xoxo

I can't concentrate on the movie now. I keep thinking about tomorrow. I need a plan for what I'm going to do after work. I'm going to need to eat supper before I go. Do I pack a supper or eat out? I ask my mom what she has planned.

I her outside watering her trees. "Mom, you are planning on coming to the fashion revue tomorrow night?"

"Of course, I am," she says, like I'm stupid.

"Well, I don't want to drive all the way home and back into town again. I can just buy my own supper somewhere and meet you there or do you have other plans?"

She thinks for a moment, then says, "What about Ben? Is he coming?"

"He's planning on it, but I don't know when he's going to be able to show up. He's bringing his friends with him, too. The people I met on the 4th and at his house."

She nods her head and says, "Then I'll just meet you there. You want me to bring anything for you?"

I'm thinking if I pack everything up: my make-up, clothes, shoes, hair stuff, I should be fine. I definitely have enough money for myself for a supper for one night, thanks to my job.

"No, I don't think so. If forgot something, I'll call you."

I go back in the house. I feel better about tomorrow, so I put in another movie and settle back down with Sbabys.

Friday morning comes faster than I want it to. I have to hurry to get ready this morning because not only do I have to get ready for work, but I also have to pack up all the stuff I need for the fashion revue tonight. I feel rushed on the drive in, but I know I will be there on time. My mind is just rushing, thinking about tonight. I get right to work and realize I'm acting like I'm running out of time. Tonight can't come fast enough. Maybe I'll be able to get two boxes done today.

By 5 o'clock, only one box remained. It was half done. I clock out and head for the exit. I'm thinking what fast food restaurant is closest to the Complex where the fashion revue is being held. A&W sounds good, so I drive there.

I decide to eat inside. I have plenty of time to eat. It's better than sitting in my car and eating. I order a burger and a hot fudge sundae.

I quickly eat. Before I realize it, it's 5:45. I have to get myself to the Complex so I can get ready. I throw my trash away and head out the door. As I'm heading out the door, my mom calls me.

"Hey, Mom. I heading over there now."

"I'm leaving as well. I was wondering if I needed to grab anything for you before I left," she said.

"I don't think so. I think I have everything. I'll see you there." I hang up the phone and get in the car.

It takes me about another 15 minutes to drive to the Complex. I grab all of my stuff and walk into the building. I go straight to the dressing rooms. There are some girls already here and getting ready. It's pretty quiet, considering how many of us are getting ready. It's nice to have some quiet time, so I slow down and enjoy it, especially since I felt rushed all day today. I find a spot next to a mirror and start changing. My hair is already half way up. I just have to add the curls. This is what takes time.

Thirty minutes later, my mom shows up. "How's it going?" she asks.

"Trying to put my make up on. How does my hair look in the back?" I ask because I didn't bring a hand mirror to see the back of my head.

My mom takes a look and grabs the curling iron. Apparently I missed some hairs.

She curls my hair as I apply my make up. "Why do you put so much on?" she asks.

I scoff. "Mom, I was in state drama this last year. I learned a few tricks on make up so I'm not washed out on stage."

I can tell she understands, and finishes my hair in silence. It's 6:45 now and all of the girls are here.

"It's time to line up!" I hear someone say.

I finish my last little touches on my make up and we all of us go upstairs to the stage. We are lined up in groups. The little ones get to go first. The seniors, which are me and some other girls, are last. While the little ones are on stage behind the curtain, ready to be called, the rest of the seniors are lined up against the wall, going up the stairs.

It seems like forever before our group finally gets called to the stage, standing behind the curtain. We watch the group before us come out from the curtain and can hear the audience clapping. It's our turn. A guy instructs us to go on. We walk out into the limelight and find our numbers to stand on. I'm the first one of the group to model since my number is one.

The announcer reads and I start modeling. "This is Jessica Brown. This is her last year so she is going out with a bang. Jessica did drama, cross-country, track, Girl Scouts as well as 4-H. This fall she is planning to go to college to be a music teacher. Good luck, Jessica."

I hear whoop-whoops and whistling as I walk back to my spot. I bet I knew who did most of that, Dave.

I feel relief now. I'm done. Now we have to wait to see if I'm completely done or if I have to do it again for state fair. The rest of the girls in my group models, then we walk behind the curtain. One more group, then we get the results.

We walk back downstairs and out the doors to the stadium where the audience is sitting. I'm trying to find Ben. I walk up along an aisle and see a hand waving. It's Dave. I walk over there, knowing Ben is there with him. Sure enough. There he is, but no empty seat for me to sit in. Not even next to Dave, so I kneel next to the chair in the aisle, which is the chair Liv is sitting in.

"You were so cute up there," Liv says.

"Thanks," I say with a smile.

Jack is, of course, sitting next to Liv. He looks at me and says, "You are so going to win." I just smile at him.

I'm trying to be quiet and crouch down low enough so people behind me can see. I wonder where my mom is. I'm looking for her. The last group is done modeling. It's time for the results. Of course, the little ones are first. They call each name for each prize, and each little girl walks up on stage to get her ribbon.

Now it's time for the seniors and their sewing. 6th, 5th, 4th, 3rd, and 2nd get called up. It seems all of us hold our breath for the first prize.

"Jessica Brown."

"Whoo!" Dave yells.

"You go girl," Liv shouts.

I walk up on stage and get my 1st place ribbon.

"And for grand prize…"

I didn't get the grand prize, but I was proud of my 1st place ribbon. We get our picture taken and walk off the stage.

Now it's time for senior modeling. I get 5th place. I'm in the top 10! I'm going to state fair! The girls that go to state fair have to go to a room for pictures and sign cards. I haven't seen Ben since they announced my win. I so much want to talk to him.

We finally get done signing cards and taking pictures. We are released to meet up with our family and friends. I'm the first one out the door. I saw Mom right there next to the door along with my dad and brother. I hug my mom and dad and fist bump my brother's hand. My mom lays her hand on my shoulder. Something's up.

"Ben said sorry. He had to take Dave and Jack back home so they can get to work early tomorrow."

"What?!"

Dad says, "Yeah, he just left. I mean just left."

I head for the doors and run outside. I can't believe I just missed him. He was just here. I look in the parking lot for his car. No sign of him. I sigh. My heart feels like it just dropped to the ground. I turn around and head back inside.

"Sorry," I say as I bump into a tall man. He doesn't move, so I look up at his face. "Bill. What are you doing here?"

The tall, skinny man looks down at me and says, "I came to watch you model. I told you I was going to come the last time I saw you. I've been wanting that second date."

I scoff.

The last time I saw Bill was the beginning of May. This was the guy that my mom insisted I go out with. Actually, Bill called the house and Mom answered the phone. Instead of asking for me, he asks my mom if it's okay to take me out on a date. My mom said yes, which obligated me to go. I was so mad at her. No one asked me.

I zig zag my way through people back to where my family was standing. Bill is following me. I get back to the spot where my family was, but they are nowhere to be seen.

I scoff again and head into the dressing rooms to grab my stuff. I take my time knowing that Bill is still out there.

After I fill my bag, I peek around the doorway to see if Bill is still there. I don't see him. I walk out of the dressing rooms, and I hear, "There you are."

I turn around and look up at the balcony, which is above the dressing rooms.

Oh, no. Landon, the octopus man.

Landon, not being a gentleman at all, jumps down from the balcony onto the main floor next to me.

"I've been looking for you. I heard that you were modeling, so came to watch. I think you should've gotten the grand prize."

I turn around and start heading out the door saying, "Thanks, Landon."

Landon follows me. "How come you never called me? I want a second date, you know." He runs past me to get in front of me.

"Sorry, Landon, but I've got to go."

I swerve past him and go outside. I start speed walking. I'm getting scared because he's running up behind me, and I'm in a dark parking lot with hardly any people around. I wonder where my family is. I quickly unlock my car, open the back seat, and throw in my stuff.

Landon caught up to me. "Where are you going so fast? Can I take you out to celebrate?" "No, Landon. I need to get home," I say as I shut the back door.

I was about to open the driver's door, but Landon got in front of me. He almost gets his arms around me but I twirl away.

"Get away from me, Landon. I mean it."

His arms are still wide open. "Hey! I just want a hug." I shake my head no. "No hug, Landon."

I start backing away and he follows.

"Come on. You used to give me hugs when we were up in the Tetons."

I shake my head to help get rid of the memories. I was so stupid going on a date with this guy.

I lead Landon far enough away from my car, then I make a mad dash around him, and I quickly get in and lock the doors. I turn the ignition on and back up, hoping I run over Landon's foot. He runs backwards to get out of my way. I speed out of the parking lot. I am going home.

Chapter 22

woke up in the middle of the night with a horrible fright. What a nightmare! I dreamt that Bill and Landon had me cornered and I couldn't get free. It's 2 am. I calm myself down and go back to sleep.

I woke up again to my phone ringing.

"Hello," I say groggily.

"Were you sleeping?" a familiar voice says.

I'm awake now. "Ben. I'm so happy to hear your voice. I'm so sorry I missed you last night. I wish I didn't have to do pictures and sign all of those cards."

"It's okay," Ben said. "Your mom told me what all you had to do to get ready for state fair. Congratulations by the way."

I smile. "Thanks, Ben."

"The whole reason I called early is because I was wondering if we could go to the fair early."

I'm rubbing my eyes to try and wake them up.

Ben continues, "To look at the exhibits like you wanted to."

"Yeah. Yeah, totally. Just give me an hour and I'll be ready."

"Ok. I'll leave in 45 minutes."

"Sounds great, Ben. Bye."

"Bye."

I flop back on my bed. Today should be great. I have an hour to get ready. I better get in a hustle. I take a quick shower and put on a teal tank top and jean shorts. I comb my hair down, add eye make up, and some stud earrings. I make and eat my breakfast, and head back in my room to finish doing my hair. It's is still pretty wet so I blow dry it down. I put a hair tie on my wrist just in case I want to put it up later.

"Hello?" I hear.

"I'm in here," I yell through the house.

I have my bedroom door open, but Ben still lightly knocks on it.

"Sorry," I say. "I had to blow dry my hair. It was pretty wet still. I'm ready though." Ben smiles and says, "Still look pretty no matter what you do."

I thank him with a kiss.

We go out the door and into Ben's car. He drives us back to the fair. On the way, I didn't say a word to him about last night. In fact, I didn't even want to talk about it, so I kept it from him.

We make it back to the fairgrounds, and Ben asks, "What should we see first?"

"I want to look at the animals first, if that's okay? Also, I didn't get to talk to Sarah much when we saw her at the carnival. I wouldn't mind trying to find her."

Ben smiles and puts his arm around me. We head back into the pig barn. We wander through the pens and look at the pigs. We comment how fat or hairy some of them are. I found Sarah's pigs, but no sign of Sarah.

"Let's look at the vendors," Ben says.

The vendors are on the other side of the pig arena. I feel sorry for them. They have to be here every day smelling pigs.

We are at the other end of the vendors and I realize I need to use the restroom.

"I'll wait here," Ben says.

I think he wanted to look at the Swiss army knives anyways, which is right next to the doors to get to the concessions and restrooms. I go through the double doors and head into the ladies room.

I come out startled because Landon came out of nowhere and was right there in front of me. "I thought you would be here today. I saw you go in, so I waited knowing you were going to come right back out!"

I scoff and go through the double doors.

"I want that second date," Landon yells after me.

I see Ben right where I left him. I grab his arm and lead him through the people and vendors and out a side door, not looking back.

"What's going on?" Ben asks.

We made it into the sunshine and I stop. I turn around to see if Landon is following. I exhale.

"Are you alright?" Ben asks.

I need an excuse. "Yeah, I'm fine. Just needed fresh air. Let's go to the exhibit hall."

I turn around again, making sure Landon isn't anywhere to be found. I take Ben's hand and lead him across the road and lawn to the building where I dropped off my skirt and jacket. Ben and I don't say a word to each other the entire walk there. I lead him to another side door and we walk in. The fiddle contest must be going because we can hear fiddles and violins playing. We watch for a little bit then we go into the next room and look at the exhibits. Everything is nicely displayed: the wood-working, posters, cookies, cake decorating, quilts, and gardening. Next, we look at the pictures. I walk a little bit ahead of Ben and round a corner to look at more pictures. Oh. I see two guys from my class. I was about to walk up and talk to them when I see what they are looking at.

Gasp Mom!

Without my knowing, my mom entered a private senior picture of me. It was just supposed to be between Mom and me. Back when Mom was taking pictures of me for my senior year, she decided to experiment with taking photos of me in the grass. I sit in the tall grass, and Mom tells me to pull my straps down because the colors would appear too bright in the picture. When my mom developed the pictures, I saw the one with me in the grass. Actually, it shocked me. I actually looked <u>naked</u> in the grass. All you could see are my face, shoulders, and the top of my chest. I am also posing with this goofy smile.

And now, this picture is up on the board for everyone to see, and two boys from my class are looking at it. I quickly slip back behind the wall. I see Ben still looking at the pictures, and he is coming my way. I grab his arm.

"Let's go look at the clothes, shall we?" I say.

Ben pulls his arm out from my hands, and says sternly, "What's with you? First you drag me out of the vendors, now you are dragging me away from the pictures. What is going on?"

I look up at the ceiling, then down at the floor.

I exhale.

I'm going to tell him. "There's a picture of me over there that my mom entered."

"So?" Ben says, still a bit agitated.

I say quietly, "I look naked in it."

Ben's eyes grew big, then he rounds the corner to look. I exhale a groan and slump my shoulders. *Why do guys have to see girls naked?*

I poke my head around the corner. Well, the guys from my class are gone, but Ben is now looking at it. I wander up to him.

He must know I'm behind him now and says, "It's not bad. It's sexy. You can't see anything."

"I know," I say quietly. "But it's embarrassing. I can't believe my mom entered it. I also just saw two guys from my class looking at it."

I'm looking at the floor. I also feel embarrassed about dragging Ben everywhere. He's right. I need to stop, so I better tell him why I dragged him out of the vendors.

I exhale, then continue. "Ben. The reason why I took you away from the vendors because 'octopus man' found me, and I didn't want you two to meet. I didn't know what you would do if you met him."

I look at Ben, and his eyes are big again. "But he didn't follow you here."

Ben is looking around now. Then he stops abruptly and asks, "How did he know you were going to be here?"

I take another deep breath. "Because I ran into him last night. Someone told him I was modeling so he assumed I was going to be here today. He assumed right."

Now Ben take a deep breath.

"Sorry," I say. "I should have told you, but I wanted to have fun today. I didn't want to talk about it."

Ben puts his hands on my shoulders and looks squarely in my face. "What happened last

night?"

"Let's get a bite for lunch, and I'll tell you all about it."

I'm thankful there is food across the room. I pay for our lunch and sit down at a table.

"Ok. Spill. Tell me what happened last night," Ben urges.

I tell Ben everything. I tell him when I ran out in the parking lot to find him and ran into Bill. I tell him about when Landon finds me and tries to hug me in the parking lot.

"Did this happen after I left?" Ben asks.

I nod, yes.

"I felt so bad for leaving. Now I feel even worse," Ben hangs his head.

I take Ben's hand. "Don't feel bad. I knew you had to take Dave and Jack home so they can get to work. I felt bad I couldn't leave the room soon enough. I guess I had just missed you. My parents said you just walked out the door when I came out."

"Really?" Ben says. "I should've stayed just two minutes longer. I'm sorry." Ben and I hug.

I feel better now that I told him everything. The weight from my shoulders has been lifted. Both Ben and I agree that from now on, he stays with me at all times until the end of the day.

We finish looking at the exhibits after lunch and head back across the road to the vendors. Ben wanted to finish looking. That's fine. I felt bad I pulled him away from them the first time. I even got to see Sarah while Ben was looking. Sarah was telling me all the shows she's been doing and the prizes she won. She still has to show her steer tomorrow. Then she gets curious about how Ben and I started dating. I told her it started with just asking for a phone number back in May. Sarah approves and hopes this relationship lasts long, maybe forever. I didn't know what to say to that other than smile. I just know Ben and I have to take it one day at a time.

After talking to Sarah, we go look at the bunnies, chickens, exotic animals, goats, sheep, and steers. There was a sheep show going on as we were browsing.

Once we are done looking at the steers, we walk around the arena to get back to the concessions and restroom area. I happen to look across the arena and see Landon. He waves at me. I go to reach for Ben to tell him, but he isn't there.

Where did he go?

I look ahead and see him walking for the double doors. Then I look back at Landon. He is coming around the opposite way to the double doors. I run to Ben, but it was too late. He went through the doors. Where is he going so fast? I was about to push the doors open to get to Ben, but Landon grabbed the door, holding it closed. He is strong. You could tell because of the muscles that are showing through his black t-shirt.

"Where are you going in such a hurry? I was just wondering who that guy was that you grabbed earlier today."

Drats! I look through the window of the door. *Ben, where are you?* I look at Landon. "He's my boyfriend."

"Boyfriend! Pshaw! I'm your boyfriend. I'm just wanting that second date. How about you and I go to the carnival and ride the rides? We can make out on the Ferris wheel." He licks his lips and raises his eyebrows.

Yuck!

Then I smile to myself, remembering Ben and I kind of already did that.

"Sorry, Landon, but I've got to find my boyfriend." I push the door really hard, out of Landon's hands. I make it to the other side. *Now, where did Ben go?*

Landon then grabs my hand and starts pulling me toward the concessions and out the door. I'm struggling to get free from Landon.

I see Ben walk out of the men's restroom.

"Ben!" I shout.

Landon then stops pulling.

Ben looks in my direction and sees Landon holding onto my hand.

"Hey! Let go of her!" Ben says as he stomps up to us.

Now everyone stops what they are doing and watches.

Landon notices and chuckles. "Hey. Just trying to get her to go on some rides with me. Just want her to have some fun, but I see she would rather be stuck here with you."

Ben takes my hand and pulls me toward him. I hug him.

Landon goes out the door.

Ben sighs. "Sorry. I really needed to use the restroom." He's still hugging me and stroking my hair.

"I'm fine now, Ben," I say.

I feel protected, but I also feel like a little kid who lost her mommy.

Ben lets go of me. "Sorry," he says. "I was just thinking what could've happened if I hadn't come out of the restroom when I did, or what I should've done differently so you didn't have to be in that situation…"

I sigh. "No matter now. Let's just get on with our lives like everybody else did."

Ben looks around and notices no one is paying attention to us anymore.

He smiles. "You're right."

He puts his arm around me, and we both walk out, past the concessions, and over to the tent.

There are lots of people sitting at the tables. I look at the board for entertainment. 3:00 - singers.

Even Ben is curious to know what's going on. "What's happening here?"

I point to the board and say, "There are some singers coming."

"Want to watch?" he asks.

"Sure."

We find a spot at a table and wait for it to start.

Chapter 23

I don't know about Ben, but I really enjoyed the show. I stand and clap at the end. Everyone else, including Ben, stands and claps as well. I sit back down and look at my phone to see what time it is. The barbeque doesn't start for another hour.

Ben sits back down and I ask, "What do you want to do now? The barbeque doesn't open until 5."

Ben thinks for a moment. "We can walk around the carnival, I suppose. We don't have to ride the rides. Just look."

"I'm okay with that," I say and smile.

We take each other's hands and walk toward the carnival. We walk around, watching people enjoy themselves at the games and standing in line for rides. Ben and I run into some people we know, so we stop and chat for a-while. All of them are surprised that we are dating. I notice that there aren't many people around now. I look toward the tent, and I see a line of people at a tiny building.

"I think the barbeque started," I say to Ben.

"Ok. I guess we better go," Ben tells the people he's been talking to.

When Ben sees the long line of people, he says, "Wow. This is a big event." We both look under the tent and it's already packed with people.

We walk under a tree. "This is a good spot to eat," Ben says, then he looks at me and asks, "Can you save this spot while I go get us something to eat?"

I nod my head yes.

Ben runs toward the end of the line. Midway, he stops and yells, "What would you like?" I yell back, "A little bit of everything!"

He turns back around and continues running to the end of the line. I sit down in the grass and enjoy the shade from the hot sun. I hear chatter from people and kids screaming and playing in the distance. The grass and dirt I'm sitting on is soft and cool from the shade. It's a nice relief from being out in the sun. The food from the barbeque is smelling really tasty. I wish I'm in line with Ben instead of sitting here being tortured by the aroma of food.

It's going to be a while before Ben gets back. I start pulling blades of grass out of the dirt. I have warm feelings. I feel so in love taken care of. I am beginning to feel hot in the cool shade, glowing from loving thoughts of how Ben takes such good care of me. I continue pulling out the blades of grass and enjoying the feelings I have for Ben. A shadow then appears next to the tree.

I look up.

Oh no. Bill.

"What are you doing here by yourself?" he asks. "Just waiting for my boyfriend to bring me my food."

Bill sits down next to me. "I can go get it for you," he says.

I look at him with a raised eyebrow. "He's coming. He'll be here soon."

I continue pulling out the grass, and Bill slithers quietly next to me. Then my stomach rumbles. I put my hand on my stomach, thinking that will hush it.

"You seem hungry, Jess. I can get you some food." Bill starts to stand up.

"No. My boyfriend is coming with the food. I can wait. It's fine." Bill sits back down, then says, "I don't think you have a boyfriend." I look at him, and say, "I do, and he's coming."

I start looking for Ben in the long line of people. I can't find him. I continue pulling out the grass, and I'm doing it now with more vigor. My stomach rumbles again. I keep pulling out grass, ignoring Bill. If it weren't for Ben wanting this spot, I would have moved by now. Instead, I keep my post. Why do I have this nasty feeling Bill's eyes won't leave me? It's creepy. I look at him, and yes, his eyes are on me.

He says, "I still don't think you have a boyfriend. Otherwise, he would be here with you right now. I know I wouldn't stand you up or leave you."

When he said, "leave you," the hairs on the back of my neck stand up. I'm kind of creeped out. I look at the grass now. I wish he would look somewhere else other than at me. I look at the long line again, hoping to see Ben.

I sigh.

Bill starts talking again. "I was wondering if I could have that second date. We could go to the carnival and ride the rides. I'll win you a big, stuffed bunny."

I look at him with my nose curled. "No thanks."

I look at the people again, watching for Ben.

Bill continues, "I know you don't have a boyfriend. You can stop lying to me. I like you, Jess. Please let me take care of you."

Finally! I see Ben walking towards the tree with two plates in his hands. I get up and run to him. I take a plate from one of his hands.

Ben notices I wasn't alone under the tree. "Who is that?" he asks.

I sigh. "That's Bill."

Ben looks at me. "And Bill is who?"

We start walking toward our spot. "Bill is the guy that my mom made me go out on a date with. Now he won't leave me alone."

Ben sighs.

Poor Ben. I wonder what he's thinking.

We both get up to the tree, and Ben says, "Hey. I had my girlfriend reserve this spot for us. Can you please find another place to sit?"

Bill looks at Ben and asks, "Who's your girlfriend?"

Ben looks at me, and quietly asks, "Is this guy for real?"

I just raise my eyebrows and roll my eyes.

Ben looks back at Bill and points to me. "This is my girlfriend, Jessica. Now, can you please move?"

Bill looks at me. I don't say anything. In fact, I look at the ground, trying to avoid eye contact with him.

Bill gets up and leaves. Ben and I sit down with our backs against the trunk.

"Man. The guys you used to date."

I look at the ground, embarrassed. "I know."

Ben probably thinks I'm not worth it anymore. He probably doesn't want a girl that he has to defend from other guys all of the time. It would be awful tiring. I poke my barbeque sandwich with my chip.

"Are you ok?" he asks.

"Oh, yeah. I'm fine." I poke my sandwich with my chip again.

"Well, you're not eating. What's wrong?"

I sigh and put the chip back on my plate. I say, "You probably think I'm not worth this. Trying to save me from other guys all of the time. I don't think you want to be in a relationship that exhausts you."

I pick the chip back up and crunch it on top of my sandwich.

"Jess." He makes me turn my head so I'm looking at him. "You are so worth it. I know why these guys want to date you. They just need to learn to move on."

I smile. I pick up a chip and put it in my mouth.

Ben speaks again. "If I have to keep reminding them, then so be it. I will. I just hope none of them hurt you." He puts his arm around me and continues eating.

I smile at him. He doesn't notice because he's looking at the crowd, but I admire him. I kiss his cheek and lay my head on his shoulder.

"You better eat," he says.

I smile and pick up my sandwich. I take a big bite. So good!

After we get done eating, we throw our stuff away in the trash bins.

"I don't know about you," Ben says, "but I'm done being around people today." I smile and say, "I agree. Take me home."

Ben smiles and takes hold of my hand and leads me through the crowd of people back to his car.

The inside of Ben's car is so hot from the sun beating down on it. Outside is much cooler than his car, so I roll down the window. He does the same, then slowly drives out of the parking lot and onto the main road. When we pick up speed, we roll up the windows and Ben turns on the AC.

I look at the time on his car. It's 7 o'clock. I don't know if he wants to stay at the house and watch a movie or go back to his home.

I look at him and ask, "What time would you like to be home?"

"Oh, I don't know," he answers. "I was hoping to watch a movie with you before I go."

I smile. "That sounds like a great plan."

Ben smiles back. His smile made me have the shivers, or was it the AC? Either way, he has a great smile. I like it when he smiles.

We make it back home. Mom and Dad and my brother are outside enjoying the sunset out on the front deck.

"Did you guys have fun?" my mom asks.

Ben and I look at each other, then we speak at the same time. "Yeah. It was fun." "It was an interesting day."

We both laugh.

Then I say, "Ben is going to stay for a movie before he goes home. Is that okay?" Dad says, "Yeah, sure. Pick a movie."

We go inside and look through the movies. As we do, Ben asks, "Your brother doesn't say much, does he?"

I scoff, and say, "You don't live with him. He's just shy around people. He'll come around."

"Didn't your brother do track?" Ben asks.

"Yeah, he did. But he only did discus and shot put. He was good at it, but I don't know why he quit."

"Maybe I'll try to talk to him some day."

I look at Ben and smile. "You're actually going to try and talk to my brother? Good luck trying to make conversation with him."

Now he is looking at me. "Is that a challenge?"

I laugh. "I'm just saying."

Ben looks back at the movies. "Well, I like you and your mom and dad. I just want to get to know your brother also."

I rub Ben's back. "Just give him some time. He'll come around."

Ben and I agree on a movie and put it in. The rest of the family comes in and joins.

"What are we watching?" Dad asks.

"*Face Off,*" I say.

"I haven't seen this in a long time," Dad says as he sits down in his recliner. Mom sits in her rocking chair. My brother takes the bean bag, and Ben and I are sitting on the couch. After a while, Dad gets up and makes popcorn for all of us.

"Some snackies," he says as he hands a bowl to Ben and me. We take the bowl and start right in. My dad brings a little bowl for my brother, and he and Mom are sharing from another bowl.

We finish the movie, and I follow Ben outside. Its chilly now, and I hug myself. Ben turns around and says, "I'll see you tomorrow morn for church."

He hugs me. I unwrap myself and put my arms around him. He's so warm, and I smell his sweat from earlier today with a hint of cologne still lingering. He still smells good. Our hug ends and we kiss. We exchange long, loving kisses for a while. Then he slides into his car and drives away. As I watch him drive down the street, I can still feel his warmth. A cool breeze blows, ending the moment and I hug myself again. Once I can't see Ben's car anymore, I head into the house, before my goosebumps make my hairs grow faster.

Chapter 24

$\mathcal{W}$e do our normal church and pizza routine again.

After pizza and the movie, Ben asks, "Do you want to come to my place this afternoon? You can follow me in your car."

This time I know I can trust Ben, and the thought of being alone with him in his house doesn't scare me this time.

I nod my head yes. "Just let me change into some shorts first."

I get up from the couch and head to my room. I quickly get out of my skirt and into jean shorts. As I come out of my room, Ben is still sitting on the couch playing with his phone.

He sees me and says, "You ready?"

I nod my head and smile.

I grab my purse and head out to the garage. He helps me push the garage door open.

"Just be home at a decent time," my mom reminds me.

Looks like she's going to do some yard work.

"I will," I say to her.

My mom hears and knows all.

Ben gets into his car and drives off. I start my car and follow him.

As he pulls into his driveway, I park in front of his house. He gets out of his car and automatically sort of runs inside. I get out of my car and walk in. I stand in the doorway, and I see Ben picking up clothes and blankets from his furniture.

"I see you need to do some house cleaning. Anything I can do to help?" I ask as I rock back and forth on my feet.

Ben picks up a shirt from the recliner, "No. You can help yourself to whatever you want to do. You can watch TV, you can take a nap. Just help yourself."

I stand in the doorway thinking and watching Ben.

"How about supper? I can go to the grocery store and pick up some food and make something while you housekeep."

Ben stops and thinks. "Yeah. That sounds good." He then continues to clean.

"Okay," I say and turn around out the door, back to my car.

As I'm driving to the local grocery store, I'm thinking… what in the world am I going to make? I want to cook something nice, yet not fancy. Steaks, potatoes, and broccoli? No. I want to make something so he can have leftovers to take to work. Maybe a casserole.

I walk into the store. What is usually in a casserole? Noodles. I go to the noodle aisle and look. I need to make something that I can whip up without using a recipe. I'm looking at all sorts of noodles. Then I run across lasagna noodles. Hmm. Lasagna sounds good. I pick up the box and turn it around. Hey, look! There's a recipe on the back on how to make lasagna. I wander throughout the store and pick up the rest of the ingredients I need using the recipe on the box for help. I pay for the food and head back to Ben's.

I walk up to Ben's house carrying in the groceries. He must have gotten hot because the screen door is open, so I let myself in. I don't see him anywhere, but I do see that he has vacuumed and swept his floors already. The place looks nice!

I wonder where he is.

I let myself in the kitchen and put the groceries on the counter.

"Ben, I'm here!" I say loudly as I take the food out the bags.

I wait for a response.

Instead, I hear rustling and I turn my head around. I see Ben carrying a huge load of clothes in a laundry basket. I think he needs one or two more baskets to carry all of those clothes, but he manages to pile it all into one. I also see he has taken his shirt off, and his biceps are bulging, carrying this pile of laundry.

"Whoa," I accidentally say.

Ben stops and says, "Huh?"

I turn my head quickly around. I'm trying to figure what to say.

"Uh, um. Don't mind me. Just keep doing what you're doing." I wave my hand at him to urge him on.

I hear Ben walk across the kitchen and around the corner. His washer and dryer must be in there. He's there for a-while, and I start making the lasagna. I start by cooking the noodles and meat sauce. I search through his kitchen to find the right sized baking pan for the lasagna. Voila! I found one. I grease it up with the shortening I bought at the store. I start laying the noodles in it. As I reach for the spoon that's in the pan of the meat sauce, I hear Ben coming out of the room. He's carrying is vacuum cleaner across the kitchen, making his muscles bulge out of his arm again. Distracting me.

"Ow!"

Instead of grabbing the spoon, I lay my hand right on the burner instead.

I'm in so much pain that I don't realize that Ben had stopped whatever he was doing to come to my rescue. I feel his sweaty arms around me, and he guides me to the kitchen sink. He turns on the cold water and puts my injured hand under it. It feels better, but it still hurts.

When he turns off the water, both he and I look at my hand. I have blisters forming on my fingertips and the bottom of my palm.

"This looks bad," he says. "I have some stuff for burns."

His right hand is around my wrist, keeping my injured hand free from touching anything, and his left arm is around my body. He leads me into the bathroom and sits me down on the toilet. He opens up his mirror, which is his medicine cabinet. He pulls a couple of things out and kneels in front of me.

As Ben dabs some ointment on my blisters, he asks, "What made you do this?" How do I answer this question? "I uh, I was uh, I was distracted."

Ben puts bandages around my injured hand and asks, "What distracted you?" He then throws the bandage wrapper away in the trash and looks at me, waiting for me to answer.

I think quickly. Instead of telling him, I will show him. I bite my lower lip. I put my uninjured hand on his right hand, which is resting on my leg. I rub up his forearm to his bicep and lightly squeeze it. Then I slide my hand onto his shoulder and do a little massage. I finish by sliding my hand down his chest and putting my hand back in my lap.

I look into Ben's eyes. For the past month, I have never seen him look at me this way. His eyes are deep pools of blue. He lifts my left hand up as if he's going to kiss it, and puts his other hand on the small of my back. He guides me off the toilet onto his lap. His face is now in my neck.

I feel him inhale and exhale.

Then he starts kissing my neck. I start feeling warm and tingly. I slide my legs further down onto his lap, and my face ends up in his neck. Ben is still kissing my neck and shoulders.

I inhale and exhale.

I can't help myself and I start kissing his neck. As I do, I notice that he stops his action. I kiss my way up his neck, behind his ear, to his cheek, then on his lips. He starts kissing me wildly and squeezing me tight against his body. He loosens his grip and starts kissing my neck again. He works his way down to my shoulder. He moves my tank top and bra strap down.

I realize what's happening now, and I get off of his lap and plop myself back down on the toilet. I put my tank top and bra strap back up to my shoulder. The warm feeling is gone now, and I feel my burnt hand throbbing again. I pull it close to me and look at Ben. His head his hanging.

He bangs his fist against the wall, then stands up and leaves the bathroom. I want to know if he's okay.

Wait.

He may be mad at me. I'm not sure what to do.

In mid-thought, he shows back up in the doorway. He puts his arms up, holding himself against the frame. His muscles are bulging again. I look, but I quickly look away hoping he wouldn't notice. I know he didn't see that because his head is hanging down again, and his leg is moving back and forth. He scratches his head. He seems fidgety.

He sighs and says, "I'm sorry, Jess. I don't want to be like those other guys you've dated."

Then he leaves.

I can tell he is mad at himself. I get up off the toilet and walk to the edge of the bathroom door. I look to my right, and it's dark. I assume that's his bedroom. I look to my left and I see the orange light from the sun on the floor. I walk toward the light, into the living room, where Ben is sitting in his recliner next to the window with his face in his hand. The sunlight is beaming down on him. To be honest, he looks gorgeous.

I gulp down my words so I don't accidentally say them out loud. I slowly start walking toward him. His fingers come off his face.

I stop, waiting for him to say something or do something.

His hand is still on his face. I see now his eyes are closed, and I continue walking toward him.

He must know I'm coming up to him because he takes his hand off his face and says, "I think you should leave."

Well, I didn't expect that! My lower lip drops and I back up into the kitchen doorway, then I realize that the lasagna is half-way made.

"I'll finish the food, then I'll leave," I say and head into the kitchen.

I complete putting the lasagna together and place it in the oven. As I do, I hear Ben walk across the kitchen, back into the room where he put his load of clothes. Then I clean the pot, pan, and utensils I used to make the lasagna. I dry them and put them away.

I round the corner and stand in the doorway, holding my injured hand close to me. It's so sore from washing.

I see a little room with the washer and dryer. I also see Ben with a shirt on now, ironing a collared shirt. I'm even surprised he knows how to iron.

I don't want to startle him, so I quietly say, "The food is in the oven. It will be ready soon."

I don't let Ben look at me. I look down on my hand and notice the bandage is almost off from doing the dishes. I rip it off all the way and toss it in the trash. I walk to the front door where my purse is. I grab it, unzip it, and take out my keys. I do this all with my left hand. I walk out of the house and down the three steps to my car. By now, tears are streaming down my face. I get in and shut the door. I place my purse on the passenger seat and start sobbing into the steering wheel.

I calm myself down and put the car key into the ignition with my left hand and turn it on. I put my foot on the brake and my left hand on the gear shift. I look up and see Ben standing in front of my car.

I think my heart went into my head.

I turn off the car with my left hand and get out. I walk to the front of my car where he is standing. He has his hands in his pockets and he is looking up and down at me.

"I see your bandage came off. Let me fix that."

He puts his arm around me and leads me back in the house.

I sit on his toilet once again, and Ben bandages me back up. He throws the bandage wrapper in the trash and plops down on the floor, slamming his back against the wall.

He sighs. "Look, Jess. I'm a guy, and…and…and you're new at this. Just…" Then he laughs.

"Just don't rub my arm that way again."

I exhale a laugh and say, "Okay."

The oven is now beeping.

Ben and I look into each other's eyes again, and he says, "I think the food is ready." He takes my uninjured hand, leads me into the kitchen, and sits me down at his little table. I hold my throbbing, injured hand close to me and watch him shut off the oven and timer.

He grabs two hot pads and opens the oven.

"Mmm. Lasagna," he says as he pulls it out.

He brings it to the table and lays it down with the hot pads. Then he goes to the cabinet and takes out two plates, opens a drawer, and grabs two forks. He places one plate and fork in front of me and places the others across the table, but there is no chair there. He goes back into his laundry room and comes back with a folding chair. He opens it and sits down, then takes his fork and cuts into the lasagna. He places a big piece on my plate and another big piece onto his plate.

He cuts into his lasagna and was about to take a bite, but I said, "Stop Ben. We need to pray first."

"Oh, right."

He places his fork down and folds his hands.

I pray, "Dear Lord, thank you for the fun weekend and the nice weather. Thank you for the food we are about to eat, and I thank you for this man that sits across from me. Amen."

I open my eyes, and Ben is looking at me, smiling.

I watch him eat his lasagna. "This is fantastic. I don't even have a cookbook in this house. How did you make this?"

I get up from my chair, walk to the garbage can, and pull the noodle box out of the trash.

I give the box to Ben with the recipe facing up.

"You're kidding me?"

I sit back down and watch him eat while he reads the box.

I sigh and look at my fork.

My right hand is injured, so I try to eat left-handed. I pick up my fork with my left hand and attempt to cut a piece of noodle. I stab it and put it in my mouth. It feels unorthodox to eat with my left hand.

"How are you doing over there?"

I look up and see he is watching me now.

"I can do this," I say.

I try cutting into the noodle again. This time I try to scoop up some meat with my noodle, and the fork slips out of my hand and onto the floor. I bend over to get it, but I see Ben is under the table with his hand already on it. Ben gets out from under the table and stands up.

I reach for my fork and say, "It's okay, Ben. Your floor isn't that dirty. I can still use it." He wipes my fork with a paper towel, pulls his chair close to mine and sits down. He

scoops up the bite I was about to eat and pops it into my mouth.

I can't help but laugh and say, "I feel like a baby."

I abruptly stop, noticing Ben didn't even crack a smile.

"But you're *my* baby."

He puts my fork down, and places his hand under my hair at the back of my head. He leans in and kisses me.

If I were butter, I would melt into this chair.

He grabs my fork again and proceeds to feed me until the big piece on plate is all gone. He picks up our plates and forks and sets them in the sink. He grabs Saran wrap from a cupboard and covers the lasagna, then he places the entire pan into his fridge.

He points to the fridge and says, "I'm taking that into work with me tomorrow." I smile and say, "I was hoping you would."

As I'm stand up from my chair, Ben rushes over, wrapping his arms around me.

It kind of surprises me.

I slide my injured hand out from in between us and hug him back.

"I love you," he whispers.

I open my eyes and realize what he just said.

I say back, "I love you too."

We continue hugging and swaying to our own music.

Chapter 25

$\mathcal{B}$ecause this is my last week of work, Monday starts off rough because my right hand hurts and is still bandaged. I try to do everything with my left hand. Of course, everyone who sees me has to ask what happened. I told the story maybe ten times today. You never realize how often you use your dominant hand until it's injured. By the time I'm ready to go to bed, my left arm is so sore that I automatically fall asleep the moment my head hits the pillow.

Tuesday, after lunch, I receive an array of spring flowers and a card.

"Is that from your boyfriend?" my boss asks.

"I don't know," I say feeling embarrassed.

I take the card out from the flowers and open it. It read, *Sending thoughts your way.*

Then below, hand written is: We hope your hand feels better. Love, Ben, Dave, and Jack.

I hug the card and smile. That is so sweet.

"Is it from your boyfriend?" my boss asks again.

"Yes, and more. His buddies."

"Aww. That's sweet."

I continue entering data into the computer. I can use my right hand again, but my fingertips really can't feel the keys because of the blisters.

This makes me make mistakes, and I'm not happy about that. Other than that, I've been trying to use my right hand more today.

I get interrupted again by my boss. "Since Friday is your last day here, can we take out you out to lunch that day?"

As she asks, she swings her finger around in the office, meaning she and two other co-workers in the office want to take me out to lunch.

I smile. "That sounds great."

After I get off work that day, I text Ben telling him that I appreciate the flowers and the card, and to tell Dave and Jack the same. I expect him to text me in his own time, but I receive a text right back.

Ben: You're welcome. How is your hand?

Me: I'm using it again today. Yesterday I couldn't. It hurt too much.

Ben: Are you changing your bandages?

Me: Yes. My mom helps me with that.

Ben: What did your parents say when they saw your hand?

Me: I just told them what happened leaving you with your shirt off out of it.

Ben: LOL. Gotta finish my job. Love u. xoxo

Me: K. Love u 2. Xoxo

I get into my car now and drive on home.

On Friday morning, I wake up two minutes before my alarm goes off. I lay in bed watching the clock, waiting for it to buzz. When it buzzes, I reach over and shut it off. I get out of bed and do my normal routine except for making my lunch. I feel excited yet sad that this is my last day of work. I'm glad I don't have to work anymore, but I'm sad because summer is almost over. I'm going to college in two weeks. Next week, I'm in Douglas.

I get myself to work and clock in like it's just another day. I head to my desk and log into my computer. I was so intent in logging in that I didn't even notice the flowers on my desk. Another array of spring flowers! I take the card out and read what was written, We appreciate all your hard work here. Good luck in your first year of college!

I look at my boss and smile, "Thank you. Thank you for the card, and the flowers, and this job. I really learned a lot."

She answers, "You're welcome. There's more to come later."

I know what she means, and I smile. I continue on with my job.

By lunch, we drive to a steak restaurant. Once we are seated in a party room, we order our drinks and look at the menus. I order a filet mignon. I never had one before, so today's the day. When I get it, I study it. It's smaller than I thought it would be. It's just a small steak wrapped in bacon. I'm thinking that this isn't going to fill me, but it's a good thing I ordered a salad and mashed potatoes to go with it.

Everyone else talks as they eat and I listen. They are mostly talking about their jobs, which doesn't relate to me at all since I just stand in front of a scanner and shredder all day.

When we are done eating, my boss pays with the company credit card. What a cool going away present! They are good people.

I say, "Thank you for this. This was really nice."

"I thought it would be a good change for you, since every day you came to work with just a sandwich and chips for lunch," she chuckles.

I smile.

We get back to M&K constructing, and we are five minutes late. No one seems to care, so I don't. I clock in for the last time and head for my desk. I enter in some data and try to finish the box of papers I started this morning.

By 4:30, my boss tells me that everyone is going home early since it was Friday and no more work needed to be done.

I tell her, "Let me finish this stack of papers then I'll head out too."

Everyone else leaves, but my boss stays behind and waits for me. I quickly scan and shred the stack of papers. Then I take the empty box back up to the attic. When I get back, I see my boss has already left.

I sigh, pick up my purse, shut the light off, and shut the door. Sweet farewell to this office. Boring, but sometimes fun!

I walk to the computer and clock out. The clock on the computer reads 4:45. I feel weird leaving early, but no one else was here. What was the point? I say good-bye to the receptionist on the way out.

"Hope I see you next year," she says.

I smile and say, "Me too."

On my way out the door, I sigh, then think to myself, *I'm done until next summer.* I turn back one more time and look up at the big red sign above the door. M&K Constructing. I give a little wave and go to my car. I drive home in silence.

After I have eaten and taken a shower, Ben texts me.

Ben: I'm off. How was your last day?

Me: Bitter sweet.

Ben: What time do I need to pick u up tomorrow?

I pause to figure it out. I still have to pack and that might take me all morning to do. It takes about an hour and a half to get down there. And then there's lunch.

Me: I still have to pack, which may take me all morning. I don't know what to do for lunch. Eat here?

Ben: That or we can eat at Hank's.

Hank's is a restaurant that is off of main road, and on the way.

Me: If that's ok. I guess come over whenever. I don't have to be there at a specific time. As long as I'm in my dorm, by 11 pm.

Ben: Wow. Ok. I'll see u tomorrow morn. ☺ xoxo

Me: Xoxo

I close my phone and flop on my bed. I still have to pack for a whole week. I feel stressed right now. Maybe if I start tonight, I can bring my stress down. I get my suitcase and toiletry bag out and start packing my clothes, make up, hair ties, hair clips, earrings, and a sweatshirt with a pair of jeans just in case it rains or gets chilly. I also have to pack soaps, a towel, and a washcloth so I can take a shower there at the dorms. I don't want to forget my toothpaste, toothbrush, and brush.

Am I forgetting anything?

Oh, yes. I almost forgot my curling iron so I can curl my hair for the fashion revue. My outfit is already on the way to Douglas, thanks to the 4-H board. I'm trying to think of anything else. I lay in my bed, thinking. I drift to Ben and tomorrow. He'll take me to the fair grounds and help me with my stuff in the dorms. We may hang out some, then he'll have to leave and go back home. It's going to be a long day for him. A three-hour trip. I fall asleep thinking about it.

The next morning, I wake up later than want to. I jump out of bed, go in the kitchen, and make and eat my breakfast. Yikes! I'm still in my jammies. Jammies! That's what I'm forgetting to take with me! I quickly throw some in my suitcase and take off the ones I'm wearing. I put my underwear on and slip on a tank top and shorts. I put my hair up in a ponytail and use some hairspray to keep any stray hairs down. I need hairspray too. I put that in my suitcase. Then I brush my teeth.

"Come on in, Ben," I hear my mom say.

What?! He's already here.

I quickly finish brushing, wipe my mouth, and rush out of the bathroom.

"You're here already?" I ask.

"I had nothing else to do at home. Is it ok?" he asks.

I nod my head, yes, and walk up to him with my arms wide open and give him a hug. "How is your packing going?" he asks after the hug. Almost forgetting, he adds, "And your hand? Can I see it?"

I hold out my right hand. He takes it and rubs the hardened blisters on my fingertips and palm.

"It's healing quite nicely. May scar, though," he says and kisses it.

"Yeah, but it will make a good story to tell people," I say trying to let him know it's not that big of a deal.

"I suppose I better finish packing. I got to make sure I'm not forgetting anything," I say. I turn around and head back to my room. My mom follows me in and hands me a garbage bag.

"For your dirty clothes," she tells me. "And this," she hands me a booklet that says *Wyoming State Fair Media Kit*.

I quickly scan it. It has a schedule of events, times of entertainment, history of the fair, and prices for parking, admission, and meals.

"Thanks, Mom," I say and hug her.

"You be careful," my mom says.

"I will," I say still hugging her.

Then I end the hug by saying, "I'll be back next week. Then I have to pack for college." Is that a tear I see in my mom's eye?

Oh. I can see she is sad that I am leaving and growing up.

I give her another hug, and reassure. "I'll be fine."

"I know you will," she says, trying to hold back sobs. I'm about to cry now, so I end the hug and quickly wipe away a tear.

I look at my suitcase and say, "I think I'm ready."

My mom wipes her tears and goes out of my room. Then Ben walks in.

"My mom did the same when I left," he says.

A couple of more tears come rolling down my face. I quickly wipe them away.

"You don't realize how fast time goes until something like this happens," I say.

"I remember when I couldn't wait till I got out of the house," Ben says, looking at the floor. "Then after a year away, I wanted to go back. I knew I couldn't though. I had to become a man on my own."

I smile. "And a great man you are, too. Your mom did a good job raising you." I kiss him.

He looks at me and says, "Can you tell my mom that?" I laugh.

Ben sits on the edge of my bed and I go back to my suitcase, inspecting it.

I sigh. "I think that's everything."

I shove it tight and start zipping it up.

I look at Ben and flap my arms a bit. "It's only 10 o'clock. What do you want to do?" He thinks. "One last walk around the loop. Let you say good-bye."

I sigh again.

I don't want to cry. I nod my head yes. Ben takes my hand, stands up, and we walk out.

Chapter 26

Ben and I walked the loop and talked. I tell him some memories I had growing up here, and he relates by telling me some of his memories.

Once we get back to the house, Ben helps me get my heavy suitcase in his car, and I place my toiletry bag next to it. I go back inside one more time to hug my family. My dad hugs me longer than my mom.

"Dad, I need to go," I say in his arm.

I'm about to suffocate.

He lets go of me and kisses my forehead.

My brother even hugs me. That doesn't happen very often.

He even walks to Ben and says, "Take care of her."

Ben smiles at him and says, "I will."

I grab my purse and look at my family. I have less than a week with them left, and I'm gone to college. I sigh and follow Ben out to his car.

We drive to *Hank's*, then grab a table and order drinks.

"You're not going to look at the menu?" I ask.

"No. I've eaten here so many times. I know what I want."

I quickly look at the menu. I think just a burger and fries are good enough for me. Ben ends up ordering the same thing I do.

After we eat, Ben asks, "Does sharing a chocolate milkshake sound okay with you?"

I nod my head violently, *yes, yes, yes*. Anything with chocolate is a definite yes for me. Ben orders it, and the waitress comes back with a large, glass cup of milkshake with two straws. I know this sounds corny, but sharing a milkshake with two straws is romantic.

After we slurp the milkshake, Ben pays at the register while I use the restroom. We still have an hour drive. I walk out of the restroom and toward the door, but I don't see Ben. I turn back around, and I see him exit the men's restroom. He takes my hand and walks me back out to his car.

The drive doesn't seem long at all. We talk the entire way. Ben talks about what's been going on at his workplace with Dave. Ben makes me laugh the way he tells his stories about Dave.

We are almost to Douglas and Ben asks, "Where do I go?"

I take the media kit out of my purse, remembering that there was a map in it. I have been here the past two years, but I don't ever remember. I tell Ben where to go using the media kit. We make a couple of turns and arrive at the fairgrounds. Ben parks where the chaperones park because it's closer to the dorms.

We get out of the car, and Ben asks, "Do you know which dorm you are in?"

I look at the buildings, trying to remember. Then I check in the media kit. I missed this card. Mom must've put this in here. I'm glad she did because it tells me which building and room I'm staying in.

look at the buildings again. "This one."

I turn around and Ben has my stuff out of the car already. I carry my purse and my toiletry bag. Carrying my heavy bag with clothes, he follows me to the dorms. We walk in and go upstairs.

I'm starting to remember where the room is. "It's this way." We walk into a long room full of bunk beds.

"Whoa. This is more like a camp, not a dorm," Ben says.

I see an empty bed and lay my stuff on it. Ben does the same. I take some bills and the media kit out of my purse and put them in my back pocket.

"Alright, we better get you out before you get caught," I tell Ben.

"Why?" he asks.

"Because this is the girls' dorm."

"Oh," and he quickly follows me out.

I take my phone out of my pocket and look at the time. It's about 1 o'clock.

"What do we do now?" he asks.

I take the media kit out and look at the schedule. Ben is standing right beside me, looking at it as well.

"There's nothing really going on right now. I guess we could just walk around and see what's here. The carnival doesn't open until 5, but you will want to head home by then."

I fold the media kit and place it in my back pocket.

Ben is looking at me and smiling.

"What?" I ask.

"Surprise!" he says.

I look at him quizzically.

"I got a hotel room for tonight and Friday night. I booked the rooms that night after your fashion revue knowing you were going to be here."

"Really?!" I exclaim and hug him.

After I hug him, I say, "This is great news. I thought I only had so much time to spend with you."

I kiss him.

"Hey, Jess and Ben."

I turn around to see Sarah. Sarah won a spot to state with her milk goat.

"Did you just get here?" she asks us.

Ben and I nod our heads yes.

"I got here this morning," she says.

"I just got done settling my goat in. Want to see?" she asks.

Ben and I look at each other, and Ben says, "We have nothing else to do." He turns to Sarah and says, "Sure."

She leads the way to her goat where there are a lot of other animals around, as well. She points to her goat and says, "There's my winner."

The white spotted goat looks clean, and so does her bedding. Also, her feeder is full.

"Looks good," I say.

Sarah looks at me and asks, "Are you coming to the Welcome dance tonight?"

I look at Ben excitedly. In the next breath, she says, "But it's just for the fair goers. I don't think Ben can get in."

My lower lip drops.

I forgot. He has to have a dorm card to get in.

"That's alright," he says. "But you two can go."

I look at him with a furrowed brow and shake my head no. I say, "I don't want to go without you."

"I think you'll be fine," he says and squeezes me with one arm. "You'll have fun."

I remember the last time I went to this dance. That's how I met my first boyfriend, Cole. The one I dated long distance and who wanted to grow old with me. I know he's going to be here also. The last thing I want is to run into him at the dance tonight without Ben. I decide not tell Ben how I'm feeling.

"I'll make sure she has fun," Sarah tells him.

"Good," and he squeezes me again with his arm.

We walk around the rest of the grounds, going into different barns, and looking at the other animals. Sarah talks most of the time, and Ben answers back. I just listen. Ben holds me in his arm the entire time. The last building we go in is where the vendors and the gardening category were. We look around for a bit. Ben seems to like the vendors. He checks them out, stopping to visit with some of them, but never buys anything.

Once we walk through the building, we leave through the back and hear the carnival music. As we turn around and look above the building, we can see a Ferris wheel and some rides with their lights on, going round and round, to and fro. Sarah, Ben and I look at each other. We seem to agree to go to the carnival without saying a word. We walk around the building and then to the games and carts with their lights on. There is more here than the county fair.

Sarah really wanted to go to the dance.

We did a really short walk around the carnival, then headed back towards the dorms where the dance is being held. Actually, it was quite a walk from the carnival to the dorms. The dance is outside, but there is a chain link fence around the perimeter. There is a guy standing at the gate checking cards.

"Well, I guess this is where I leave you," Ben says.

"Can I walk you to your car?" He shrugs then looks at Sarah.

Sarah says to me, "I'll wait for you inside."

I take Ben's hand and walk him back to his car. We kiss each other good night, and I watch him drive away. I feel like my protection is gone. I have to face Cole by myself. I don't think he's going to be like Bill and Landon though. I'll soon find out.

Walking back to the dance, my phone rings. I don't know this number, but it's local, so I answer it.

"Hello?"

A male voice speaks. "How come you don't want to date me anymore? I've waited so long, and you cut me deep."

"Who is this?" I ask.

"She doesn't even know who this is." He's obviously talking to someone else now, and the speech is a little slurred. "It's me, Landon."

"Seriously, Landon. There's more important stuff I want to do than talk to you drunk," I say.

I guess he hands the phone to somebody else because a new male voice speaks up. "You cut my friend deep. You should be sorry. You better watch your back."

Then the phone goes dead. I ignore the threat because they're drunk. They probably won't even remember calling me.

When I get back to the dance, I show my card to the man at the gate, and he lets me in. I see Sarah standing next to the D.J., dancing. Watching her dance makes me smile. She looks over at me.

"Jess!"

I walk over to her and we start dancing together. The song ends and a country song comes on. It's the type of song you would want to jitterbug to. I wonder if Ben knows how to jitterbug... because I do. Then I feel a hand tap me on the back. I turn around and I see no one. I turn back around and I see a little boy in front of me.

"Want to dance?" he asks.

"Sure," I say smiling.

So cute!

I dance with the little guy until the song ends. Then I crouch down so I'm looking at him squarely and say, "Thanks for the dance, little man."

The boy blushes.

I smile and walk to Sarah.

"Did you see that?" I ask her.

"What? You mean dancing with that boy. Yeah." "Isn't that so cute?" I ask.

"Yeah. It was cute," she says with no enthusiasm.

"What's up?" I ask.

"Cole is here."

I knew it.

Sarah continues, "He saw you dancing. In fact, he's coming up to you now." I turn around and Cole is right there.

"Cole. Hi."

"Hi," he says.

Another girl, named Jamie, shows up and starts dancing with Sarah. Then she sees us and says, "Oh. You guys are still together. That's so cute."

I shake my head no.

"No? Why did you guys break up?"

Cole didn't say anything, so I said, "The long distance was too much."

Then Cole leaves.

I sigh.

He didn't complain or ask for a second date… or anything. That was easy. Feeling relieved, I start dancing with Sarah and Jamie. We danced till the D.J. said that was enough for the night.

By 11 pm, and we are all in the dorms getting ready for bed. I was one of the first ones under my covers. I'm exhausted. I fall asleep when all the lights shut off.

Chapter 27

I wake up with my phone ringing.

I answer it with a groggy, "Hello?"

"Sounds like you stayed up late last night," a familiar voice says.

I sit up in my bed. "Hi, Ben. How are you?"

"I'm good. I slept well."

I rub my eyes. I wonder what time it is. I see Sarah is already gone. "I'll let you get ready," he says. "I'll wait for you at your door." My eyes are open now. "Are you here already?" I ask. He slowly answers, "Yeah."

"I'll be down there soon," I say as I shoot myself out of bed.

I close my phone and look at the time: 8:30. I dig out a tank top, shorts, and clean underwear from my suitcase. Most of the girls are still sleeping, so I quickly dress myself in the dark. I am careful to be quiet. I grab my toiletry bag and run into the bathroom. I brush my teeth, brush my hair, wash my face, apply some eye makeup and put on deodorant. I feel I have no time to shower, so I also spray on perfume. I put my toiletry bag next to my bed, grab some money and the media kit, and run downstairs. I see Ben sitting on the steps outside the door.

"I'm sorry," I say. "We stayed till the end last night."

"That's alright," he says as he puts his arm around me. "You must've had fun." I nod my head yes.

"I knew you would," he says. "Let's go get something to eat. I'm hungry."

I laugh and put my arm around him while leading him to the cafeteria, which is right next door.

I don't have to pay for my meal because I have a dorm card, but Ben is going to have to pay. Instead, I pay for Ben's breakfast without him noticing. We find a seat at a table.

"Anything exciting happen last night?" Ben asks.

"Not really. Just danced my booty off."

"Any boys dance with you?" Ben must be curious.

I smile, remembering the little boy. "Yeah. Actually, a little boy asked for a dance. It was really cute."

"Aww," he says, then takes a bite.

I sigh and say, "But before the dance I got a phone call. Basically, right after I said good-bye to you."

Ben stops eating and looks at me. "Must not be a good call... the way you are saying

that."

I nod my head and start in the details about the threat, "I wouldn't get too worried though because they were drunk. I don't think they'll even remember calling me."

Ben sighs and sticks another bite in his mouth. Then he says, "I would stay alert this week. Make sure you are with somebody at all times, like Sarah."

I nod my head, understanding what he is talking about.

I notice people getting ready on a little stage. They are sitting up chairs, music stands, and taking fiddles and violins out of cases. I take the media kit out and have a look.

"At 9:30, the fiddle contest is going to start," I say and show Ben.

He peeks in the kit, then at the people on the stage. "Stay for a little bit and watch while we eat?" he asks.

I nod my head yes.

I look back into the book to see if there is anything else we can do today before Ben as to leave. I see once again that the carnival doesn't open until 5 pm. He has to leave before then to get home at a decent time. I hang my shoulders and look at Saturday to find that it opens at 11 that day. Maybe we can go on Saturday.

We had a good seat, and Ben and I finished eating and watching. They are good, but after a-while, it was a little boring. If you've heard one fiddle, you've heard them all. Ben asks to see the media kit and I hand it to him. He flips through it.

"Not much else going on till tomorrow," he says.

"Yeah, I know," I reply.

"Let's just walk around then. Hang out, relax, and get some sun. We will entertain ourselves today," he suggests.

I smile, then say, "As long as I'm with you, I'll always have some sort of adventure." Ben laughs and says, "I think that way about you."

We put our dishes away and did exactly what Ben suggested.

We walked and talked. We even rested on a hillside, watching people. When we got hungry, we ate. We never kept track of the time. We just enjoyed each other until it was time for Ben to go.

I walk him back to his car, and we hug for a very long time.

During our hug, Ben says, "I love you, and you stay safe this week."

I squeeze him tighter, letting him know I heard him. Then I say, "I love you too, and you drive safely."

We kiss, and I watch him drive away.

The sky is turning orange, and the sun is beginning to set. I remember that the cafeteria is going to close soon, so I head over there to get some supper, and then I go back to the dorms. I haven't showered in two days, so that's at the top of the list. I take a shower the moment I get to the room. Afterward, I lay in bed and drift off to sleep.

On Monday morning, I wake up slowly. Before I get out of bed, I take a look at the media kit to see if there is anything interesting going on today. There's nothing really, so I just lay in bed, thinking about what I can do today?

"Missing Ben?" Sarah asks, interrupting my thoughts.

"Actually, I was trying to figure out what to do today. I can't even go look at the exhibits because it's judging day."

I bring my knees up so I can hug them.

"You can hang out with me today," Sarah says.

"Can I?" I ask excitedly. "I would love that. Just let me get ready first," seeing that Sarah is ready for the day.

I think she gets up early to feed and take care of her goat.

I get ready and ask if Sarah has eaten breakfast. She shakes her head no.

"Great! I have somebody to eat with today," I say, thinking out loud.

We go to breakfast together and I end up following her around the rest of the day. Every now and then, we would check on her goat, which is understandable. One of those times, I remember that the goat show was yesterday. "How did you and your goat do yesterday?"

Sarah says that they did well, but not good enough to win anything. "Her bag wasn't big enough," Sarah says.

"I'm sorry," I reply.

I don't know anything about goats, but I thought her goat was pretty.

During the day, I only saw Cole once. He was sitting next to an exhibit hall. I'm assuming he was guarding the doors so no one could get in other than the judges. I just turn my head and keep walking with Sarah.

The day went faster than I thought it would. I'm glad, and I had fun with Sarah today. I told her about my summer with Ben and my job. She asks about Kendra, and I told her she doesn't get service where she is. I can't talk to her unless she calls me. We talked all day, even after supper and showers until it was time for Sarah to go to sleep. She has to show her goat first thing in the morning again, so she goes to sleep at a decent time. I stay awake, thinking about Ben until I fall into slumber.

The next morning, I wake up at a decent time, but I know I will be by myself for a few hours because Sarah is showing her sheep all morning. She didn't notice, but I watched her rush out the door. She was dressed up in her white shirt, black pants, and sparkly belt.

I hug my knees again, feeling a little lonely. I look at my media kit to see if there was anything else going on today. Other than Sarah's goat show, nothing really worthwhile to see. I do want to see the exhibits though, but I don't want to do it by myself because I remember what Ben told me. Still, there are some things I need to do myself like get ready for the day for one. Two, I'd rather be out and about than being stuck in the room. And three, I can watch Sarah's show for a bit. I have my plan for the morning.

After breakfast, I walk into some of the exhibit halls and look around. One is still closed for judging. Then I head over to the goat arena and watch the show until it's time for lunch. I eat with Sarah.

"At least you placed this time," I tell her softly. I can sense her disappointment.

"Yeah, but its 6th place," she says, like it's a bad thing.

I quiet down and finish eating, letting her dwell on her 6th place ribbon.

After lunch, we go back to the dorm so Sarah can change her clothes. Instead of going in, I sit on the outside steps and wait. I think, *This is the spot that Ben sat when he was waiting for me.* I smile. Across the way, I see Cole walking to the men's dorms. I watch as he walks across the lawn. He notices I'm watching him and stops to look at me. I turn my head away, but I roll my eyes back in his direction. He starts walking again and goes into the dorm. I'm glad he's not like Bill and Landon.

Sarah walks out and asks, "Ready to have some fun?" She shakes her body.

I smile because of her enthusiasm and say, "Yes. Let's!"

We walk through the animal barns again. A group of guys are hanging around the steer barn and they decide to follow us for a bit.

Sarah finally turns around and says, "You want a piece of this?" The guys stop and laugh.

We continue walking and one of the guys ropes my feet. I tripped, but didn't fall.

I turn my head and say, "Hmpf. Missed. Maybe you should keep practicing on your own feet since they're closer to your small heads."

Sarah goes, "Ooooh. Burn!"

Then we walk away. The guys take the hint and leave us alone.

For a change of pace, instead of eating supper at the cafeteria, we eat at the carnival. Afterward, we head back and shower, to refresh ourselves by getting the sweat off. It was a very hot day today.

"They're having another dance tonight. Want to come?" Jamie asks.

"Sure!" Sarah says.

I'm not so sure because of the threat I got and Ben's request for me to be safe.

"I rather be in here tonight," I tell them.

"You party pooper. It's because of Ben, isn't it?" Sarah says.

"No," I sigh.

"What's wrong?" asks Jamie.

"Is it Cole?"

"No."

"Then what is it?" Sarah asks.

I tell them, "I got a threatening phone call before the first dance, so I rather be someplace safe."

"I'll keep you safe," Sarah says.

"I know you will. That's why I plan on hanging out with you this week." I hug my knees. I feel like I'm using her instead of being her friend. "Just come," Jamie says. "It's more fun when you come."

I smile for the compliment. I sit and think: What would Ben want me to do? What if I do end up in trouble? There are a lot of people there, so no one can harm me without someone else interfering. If I need to do something alone, like using the restroom, I'll bring Sarah or Jamie with me.

"I'll go," I say.

"Yes!" Jamie and Sarah exclaim.

"But!" I yell. "If I need to use the restroom, one of you is coming with me." "Deal," both of them say.

The dance tonight was like the other night. We danced to almost every song, and when it ended, we headed back to the dorms and as soon as my head hit the pillow, I was asleep.

Chapter 28

$\mathcal{M}$ost of us sleep in this Wednesday morning. In fact, we were almost late getting to breakfast, and the cafeteria closes at 9 o'clock. After breakfast, I go back to the dorms to finish getting ready for the day. As I check out my media kit to see if there is anything interesting going on today, I notice that the beef show is at 1:00, and the carnival opens at 11.

Jamie and Sarah obviously see that I'm looking at the kit, and Jamie asks, "Does anyone want to go to the carnival today?"

"I would love to as soon as I check on my goat," Sarah says. I was hoping to do the carnival with Ben on Saturday, but I guess I can go again.

"Sure," I say as I lay the media kit on my bed.

I grab the last of my bills from my purse and stick them in my back pocket. I may have to visit an ATM.

Jamie, Sarah, and I walk over to Sarah's goat first. It's so hot out that I'm sweating from just walking in the sun. Jamie and I wait in the shade as Sarah waters her goat. Then we walk over to the carnival. We are a little bit early, so we walk around, watching and waiting for the ticket booths to open. Once we see one open, we all buy wrist bands and head for the rides. A couple of hours later, we are starving, and we eat at the carnival because we don't want to walk all the way back to the cafeteria, then back again. I thought I saw Landon round a corner at one time, but I don't think it was him. If it was, he probably would have come over to bug me.

At about 3 o'clock, Sarah has to water her goat again. Jamie and I follow and watch her take care of her goat. We decide to go back toward the dorms. Instead, the entertainment catches our attention, so we find a seat and watch.

It was another hypnotist. This guy is entertaining, and we see one of our own on stage.

After that, we talk to the girl from our club who just got hypnotized. Her name is Kim. Jamie asks, "How do you feel, Kim?"

Kim answers as she's rubbing her back, "It feels like I was sleeping on a board."

We all laugh because the hypnotist made her into a board and walked on her as she was propped up between two chairs.

Kim looks confused and says, "What?"

Jamie tells her what happened.

"No way," she exclaims.

We talk some more about it on the way to the cafeteria to get supper. Now that there are four of us, I can hardly get a word in, so I just sit and listen.

After supper, Sarah and I feel exhausted, so we head back to the dorms. Jamie and Kim still want to walk around the grounds. I take a shower and lay in bed. I missed a text from Ben, while I was in the shower.

Ben: How's it going down there? Having fun?

Me: I am having fun. Went to the carnival today with some friends.

Ben: Good. Anymore threats?

Me: No. No one has been bugging me. I'm enjoying it.

Ben: I'm glad. Can't wait to see you Friday?

Me: I can't wait either. I miss you.

Ben: Miss you too. Xoxo

Me: Xoxo

Sarah is watching me text and asks if it was Ben. I smile and nod my head yes.

"You are so in love," she says.

"I am," admitting it.

Sarah is obviously tired because within minutes she falls asleep. I turn the lights off and crawl into bed myself and effortlessly fall asleep.

The next morning I get up early. I have to model in front of the judges, so after breakfast, I get my outfit out of the exhibit hall and hitch a ride to the school. I finish getting myself ready there, which is just applying my make-up and putting on my outfit. I curled my hair this morning before breakfast. I was at the school all morning, not only because I had to wait my turn to model, but because I had to wait for Kim to get done modeling as well because she was my ride. I don't think I modeled as well as I did at the county fair, but I did the same exact thing. I think I was just missing my inner sparkle.

By the time we get back, it's time for lunch, and I'm hungry, but I can't eat in my outfit. I'm afraid that I might spill something on it. So I quickly change into a tank top and shorts, put my outfit back in the exhibit hall, and head to the cafeteria. By now it's close to 12:30, and I'm starving because I had an early breakfast. I eat lunch and head back to the dorm to look at my media kit. The steer show is today at 2:00. I might go watch that for a while since I missed yesterday's show. I look for Sarah at the goat barn and ask if she wants to watch the steer show with me. She says yes. I watch her finish putting fresh bedding in for her goat, and we walk to the next barn.

The show hasn't quite started yet, but we look at the possible winners. Then we find a seat in the stands and watch for a bit. While I'm sitting and watching the show, I see Cole walking outside the barn. It looks like he's looking for someone or something. He stops, looks behind, turns and looks into a barn, then turns and looks into the barn where we are. Apparently he doesn't seem to find whatever he's looking for and walks on. I shrug it away and continue watching the show.

Sarah gets bored after a while, so we walk back toward the entertainment. Another hypnotist show is about to start. I decide to get hypnotized again.

At the end, I wake up to a snap! And walk back over to Sarah in the stands.

"You are so funny," Sarah says.

"Yeah?" I say as I rub my eyes.

I felt like I had a good sleep, but I also had dried up tears around my eyes. I wonder… Sarah tells me all about when I was dancing and played with my dog. Then my dog got run over.

"That's mean," I say.

"I know," Sarah says. "You were crying."

So that's why my cheeks felt hardened with salty water.

We go to the cafeteria for some food. I feel wide awake now and want to walk around some more. Sarah agrees. It's getting dark, so the lights on the lampstands are on. The sky is painted black and blue in the east, and in the far west, the sky is pink, yellow, and orange. It's finally cooling down, which makes me feel a lot better. After the nap and supper, the cool evening air just gives me more energy, so we decide to stroll the perimeter of the grounds. As we walk, we talk about our summers. When we get to the secluded area of the grounds, the hairs on the back of my neck start standing up. I turn around and start walking backwards to see if I could see anything or anyone. I thought I saw a shadow run behind a barn, but it could've been kids. I turn back around and start speed walking.

"Anything the matter?" Sarah asks.

"Just a little freaked out," I say and start running towards the dorms where there are people again.

Sarah finally catches up to me. Panting, she says, "You don't think you're being followed, do you?"

I turn back and look, "I don't know, but something just didn't feel right to me. I'm going to go back to the dorms and head to bed."

"I'm right behind ya'," Sarah says, literally walking behind me.

I wake up in the morning smiling. It's finally Friday! Tonight, I get to see Ben. During the day, I hang out with Jamie, then Sarah. At some point, I asked Kim if I can have a ride back to the high school, but I tell her I won't need a ride back to the dorms because Ben is going to do that.

The moment the cafeteria opened for supper, I ate. I wanted a head start to get ready because Kim said she wasn't going to leave until 6:30, and the show started at 7. After I eat supper by myself, I rush to the exhibit hall to grab my outfit. I accidentally run into Cole as I walk in.

"Oh. Sorry, Cole. I didn't see you there."

"That's okay," he says as he blushes, and quickly moves on.

I sign my outfit out and head back to the dorms to get ready. I curl my hair, put my make up on, and put on my outfit.

By now its 6:30, and I'm waiting for Kim. She finally enters the lobby where I'm waiting. She has her outfit on also.

"I was hoping you got ready here, too. I don't like getting ready at the school," she says as she comes down the stairs.

"That's understandable," I say and follow her to her car.

As she drives there, I'm texting Ben.

Me: I'm on my way. I'll c u after I model. Save a chair for me. I'll text u when I'm in the audience, so I can find u.

Ben: Sounds good. I'm already here. xoxo

Me: xoxo. ☺

Since this is state fair, the groups are organized by counties going in alphabetical order, and we are group number 3. After I model, I am anxious to text Ben. I grab my purse from the locker room and head back to the stadium where the audience is sitting. As soon as I get there, I pull out my phone.

I text Ben: Where r u sitting at?

He texts me his seat number.

I look at the rows as I'm walking. I find the row and turn in, excusing myself as I pass in front of a bunch of people. I finally see Ben with an empty seat next to him. I also see a pretty blonde girl sitting on the other side of him. She watches me as I sit next to Ben.

I can't help but ask, "Getting hit on, were you?"

"Not that I noticed," Ben whispers back.

"I bet you were and you had no idea." I look at the girl again, and instead of watching the show, she's looking at Ben.

"I think she likes you," I whisper back to Ben. He turns and looks at her.

She smiles.

Ben scooches closer to me, then whispers in my ear again, "Can I switch places with you?"

I giggle as we exchange seats.

The blonde girl pouts.

I smirk.

Ben and I hold hands through the rest of the show.

Finally, it's time for the results. They announce girls for ribbons on stage for modeling

and sewing. Unfortunately, I didn't place. Afterward, Ben and I walk out of the stadium.

"I have to use the restroom," Ben says.

We walk hand-in-hand through the school, trying to find the restroom. We find one, and I wait outside the door for Ben. I'm leaning against the wall facing the door, when I hear a voice.

"Too bad you didn't win tonight. You should've." I turn around and it's Landon.

"What are you doing here?" I ask loudly, hoping Ben would hear me.

"I came to see you of course. I knew you would be here," he says calmly.

Without warning, he grabs my wrist and starts dragging me towards the main doors.

"Ben!" I shout.

"Oh, pretty boy won't be able to help you. My buddy took care of him in the bathroom. You know, the one you talked to on the phone."

I look at Landon.

Fear and anxiety are going through my body. I wonder what his friend did to Ben. I really hope Ben is okay.

Apparently, I make it easier for Landon to drag me because before I know it, we are at the main doors and Landon pushes them open. I'm struggling hard now to get free, but his grip is stronger than it was at the county fair. Then he throws me outside. I catch myself from falling. I now see two guys in front of me, Bill and Cole.

"What...?" I exhale.

Landon comes around me. "I have been watching you since I ran into you that day at the county fair. That's when I found Bill."

Landon walks up to Bill. "I learned a lot about Bill that day," Landon says as he brushes up against Bill and walks behind him. "Knowing you were going to be here at state fair, we followed you here. Then that's where I met Cole. I saw him with you at the dance, and I got curious. He's been my spy ever since."

I gasp.

I think to myself, *That's why I've been seeing Cole at least once a day, and that day I was watching the steer show, I saw him looking for someone. That someone must have been me.*

"You broke our hearts and we want payback," Landon says as he rounds back to me.

The word "payback" got spit in my face, he was so close.

I wipe it away, then I whisper, "What are you going to do?"

Landon walks back behind me and grabs both of my wrists and puts them behind my back like I'm handcuffed. I gasp. He is hurting me now. Then he leans in next to my ear and whispers, "Break your heart."

He straightens back up and says to Bill and Cole, "Let's go."

Bill and Cole turn around and start walking out to the dark parking lot. Landon starts shoving me forward with my wrists still behind my back. I'm scared now and start breathing heavily.

I tell myself to calm down and think of how to get out of this. I don't remember in karate how to get out of a hold when your hands are behind your back. My phone is in my purse, which is behind me on my wrist. Landon has hold of it and is squeezing the strap against my skin, which is giving me a burn.

I'm freaking out again. I don't know what to do, and I don't know what they're going to do to me. I'm so scared. I start screaming, "Help! Somebody help!"

"Shut up!" Landon yells and yaks on my wrists. The purse strap starts to hurt my wrist.

I start crying and realizing I need to pray. I shut my eyes and start praying.

"Let her go!" a familiar voice says.

I open my eyes. Is it really him?

Landon swings me around in such a way that Landon and I are facing Ben. He looks at with me with sorrow, then looks at Landon with anger.

"Let her go!"

"I see you were able to get out," Landon says. "What about my buddy?" Ben smiles and says, "Jokes on him. Let her go."

"Sorry. Can't." Landon says, then swings me back around and shoves me on forward.

I see Bill and Cole are way ahead of us now. I can barely see them. "Hey, bozos! The car is on the left!" Landon yells to Bill and Cole.

They seem to hear him and turn left. Ben runs ahead of Landon and me, which stops Landon in his tracks.

"Listen, pretty boy. You're wasting my time. The sooner I leave with her, the sooner you can have her back. She'll be broken, but you can have her back by morning."

Landon tries to go around Ben, but Ben dances with us. He is not letting us go any further. I look behind Ben and I can't see Cole or Bill anywhere. It's just the three of us. The odds are getting better.

Landon sighs then yells, "Move! I'll bring her back. I promise. Just let me finish my job!"

And with one big push on me, we get around Ben.

Apparently Ben grabs Landon because we abruptly stop, and Landon says slowly and firmly, as if threatening, "Let go of me."

Ben speaks firmly back, "No. Let go of her. Then I will let go of you." Landon lets go of me. I rub my burn on my wrist.

Ben says, "Jess, run."

Run? Run where?

I start running back towards the school. This parking lot is incredibly big. I'm almost inside the school, but what about Ben?

I turn back around. I now see Landon facing towards the school, and Ben is standing in front of him. I can see from a distance that Landon is keeping his eye on of me.

Ben and I just can't get away from Landon. We need help. The best thing I know to do is call 911. I take my phone out of my purse and dial.

"What's your emergency?" a lady says on the other side. "My boyfriend and I are being attacked. We need help." "Where are you?" she asks.

"In the high school parking lot," I answer.

"Are you able to give me your name and number?" "Yes." I give her my information.

"We will be there as soon as possible," she reassures me.

I'm watching Ben and Landon the entire time I'm on the phone. Words are exchanging but I can't hear. I just see Landon's mouth moving. Then I see Landon take a few steps past Ben. I get myself ready to run, but as soon as Landon takes two steps, Ben grabs his arm. Simultaneously, Landon twirls around and punches Ben in the face. I gasp and put my hands on my mouth.

Ben is face down on the ground, kicking his legs. Landon starts stomping towards me.

Anger is building in me. I stand my ground. My hands are turning into balls of rocks. Landon is right in front of me. I'm going to let Landon make the first move.

He grabs my left wrist. Right after he did, I bring my arm back, making his arm straight. I take my right elbow and hit him in the arm, making his arm bend the wrong way. He screams in pain and is bent over. He is exactly right where I want him. I karate roundhouse kick him in his face and he falls to the floor.

"That's for Ben," I say and step over him.

He's moaning and groaning on the ground.

I run over to Ben, who is now lying flat on the ground, not moving. I roll him over on his back.

Gasp

Blood is everywhere on his face. I almost cry at the sight. I put his head on my lap. Then I see blue and red flashing lights. Sirens are heard. I look up and see a firetruck coming to the front of the school. It makes a screeching halt right in front of Landon.

I stifle a laugh. The fire truck almost runs him over.

I get out my phone from my purse and open it up, letting it light up. I wave my phone letting the officer know where I am. He obviously sees me and drives over. The ambulance follows.

The officer comes running out with his flashlight and places his hand on me. "Are you okay?" he asks.

"I'm fine, but he's not," I nod to Ben on my lap.

The driver of the ambulance runs over to Ben. He pries Ben's eye open.

"He got hit in the head hard and may have a broken nose," he says. "Keep him awake," he tells me as he gets up and runs back to the ambulance.

I do what I am told. I take Ben's hand in mine and say, "Ben, you have to stay awake. Help is coming. Stay with me."

Ben tries to open his eyes but can't because the officer's flashlight is shining right in his face.

Ben stops trying, but says, "Jess?"

I feel his hand squeeze mine.

The driver comes back with help and a stretcher. One medic is at Ben's head, and the other is at his feet.

"On the count of three. 1, 2, 3."

They pick him up and put him on the stretcher.

I stand up, trying to get feeling back in my legs. I look back at Landon, and I see the fireman crouched down with one hand on Landon and the other on his phone.

"Ok. Tell me what happened," the officer says as he directs me to his car.

I tell him everything from when Landon dragged me out to when I kicked him in the face.

The whole time I'm talking, he is writing on his notepad.

When he gets done, he points at me with his pen and says, "You were smart letting him make his move first otherwise I would've put you in jail."

My eyes grew big, but then a sense of pride grew inside of me.

I look around and see everyone else is gone except for me and the officer.

I stop the officer from closing the door. "I'm sorry, but my ride went away in an ambulance. Do you mind giving me a ride to the hospital?"

The officer looks at me for a long minute, then decides. "I suppose. Get in."

He closes the door, and I run around the other side and get in the passenger seat. I've never been in a cop car before. Kind of exciting.

$\mathcal{W}$e make it to the hospital, and the officer walks in with me to the front desk of the emergency room. He doesn't say anything, and I don't know what to talk about.

I gulp down and say, "Ben Miller, please?"

The lady at the desk looks at the papers scattered on her desk.

"I don't see any Ben Miller," she says to me.

I gulp down again and say, "Well, he came here in an ambulance."

"Oh, well, that's different. Let me go in the back and see."

She turns around and goes through a door.

I turn and look at the officer. He says, "I think you'll be ok here. I'm going to type up this report." He taps his notebook with his pen, meaning he's going to type up my story. Then he turns and leaves, smiling.

I smile and turn back at the desk. I rest my elbows on the table and tap it with my fingers.

She comes through door. I stand up straight, taking my elbows off of the desk.

She says, "He's stable, but they have to do tests on him. You're going to have to wait." She points to the waiting room.

I look and sigh. Then I look back at the lady and give her a smile.

I walk into the waiting room. There is a couple there sitting and the T.V. is playing. I find a seat and sit down. I don't mind the time. All I know is that it's late and I'm tired. I shut my eyes and toss and turn in my chair till I find a comfortable spot. Then I fall fast asleep.

I wake up with a hand touching me. "Ma'am. He's ready and in the recovery room."

I sit up straight and rub my eyes. I'm still tired.

I look at the time. It's 4 am.

The lady from the desk is waiting for me at the doorway. I get up and follow her. She leads me to the elevators. Once we get in, she pushes 3, and we go up. It seems like we go through a maze of hallways before we finally make it to Ben's room.

The room is really bright. I blink my eyes so I can get used to the light. I walk in and I see Ben lying in bed asleep. His face his clean, but his nose is bandaged. He also has an I.V. in him and a hospital gown on.

I turn to the lady and ask, "Why an I.V.?"

She answers, "For fluids and pain medication. He's going to wake up with a really bad headache."

I nod my head.

The lady speaks up, "Do you want me to get you anything?" Now that she mentions it, my throat is dry.

"Some water please."

She leaves and shuts the door behind her.

I watch Ben as he breaths. His chest goes up and down. I wonder if he's having a hard time breathing through the little holes in his cast. I look around the room. There is a box sitting on the window sill. I look inside. It's Ben's clothes and shoes.

The lady comes back with a hospital cup. It has ice water in it. I gulp it down.

"Anything else I can get you?" she asks.

I shake my head no with a mouthful of water. Then I swallow. "No, thanks."

She smiles and turns off all the lights. I sit the cup down on Ben's rolling table, and I quietly walk to use the bathroom. I'm trying so hard not to wake him up. After I'm done, I pull the chair that was sitting under the window next to Ben's bed. I sit down in it and slowly put my hand on his hand, trying not to startle him awake. I double check to make sure I didn't accidentally wake him. No movement. Just quiet slow breaths. I lay my head down next to Ben's and my hand and fall asleep.

I wake up with Ben's hand moving out from under mine. I sit straight up and watch him. He stretches and looks around the room. Then he sees me and smiles. I smile back. His smile ends, and he makes a groan. He rolls to his side and sits up, placing his feet on the floor and placing his hand on the I.V. stand.

I quickly get up and bet around his bed saying, "Whoa. Where are you going? You need help?"

I place my hand on his back.

He quietly says, "I have to use the bathroom."

I back away and let him go in himself. I go back to my seat and wait. I hear him flush the toilet and run the water in the sink. He comes back out and walks his I.V. back to his bed. He keeps his gown closed as he gets back into bed and covers himself with the blankets. He seems to know what he is doing.

I ask, "You've done this before?"

"Yes. When I had my appendix out."

That jogs my memory. "That's right. You were gone for a long time that one year during track season. I missed you."

"Did you?" he asked. Then his eyes grew big. "How did you escape last night?" "Oh," I exhale and look down at the floor.

How should I say this quickly without repeating the story? "I kicked his butt." Ben scoffs. "No way. You beat up the guy that did this to me?"

I blush. I don't mean to make him feel weak.

"What did you do?" he asks.

I might as well tell the story. "Well, I got mad when I saw him punch you, so when he grabbed me again, I jabbed my elbow into his arm, then roundhouse kicked him in the face. I hope I broke his nose."

"Geez," Ben says then looks away.

I don't want to talk about it anymore, and I'm wondering how his head is feeling. That lady said it was going to hurt real bad this morning.

I ask, "How's your head?"

Ben looks back at me, rubs his forehead, and says, "There's pain there, but nothing to serious."

I nod my head, then my stomach rumbles. I wonder... The door opens up and a nurse walks in.

"I'm glad you're up," she says and turns on the computer next to Ben's bed and types.

"How are you feeling?" she asks.

"A little headache," Ben says.

She types into the computer.

"I need to check your vitals," she says.

"Oh, yes," Ben says. "All the time, day and night." "That's right," the nurse agrees.

I hide a giggle behind my hand.

She wraps the blood pressure around Ben's arm and pumps. Then she checks his pulse and ears. She also takes his temperature.

After she's done, she types the information in the computer again. Then she takes her blood pressure wrap and puts it around her neck, gathers her strobe and thermometer off of his bed, and says, "I'll get the doctor to come and see you as soon as I can."

She leaves. Now I can ask what I was going to ask earlier.

"Ben, sweetie, are you hungry? Do you want me to go down and get breakfast? I'm hungry."

Ben's face lights up, "Would you? That would be great!"

I get up and head for the door. I stop short at the foot of the bed, realizing I don't know what he wants to eat.

"What would you like to have?"

"The works," he says. "Pancakes, eggs, bacon, sausage..." Wow. Hungry fellow.

I slip out the door and find my way back to the elevators. When I exit the elevator, I see the directory sign on the wall: emergency room, laboratory, waiting room, gift shop, admission, cafeteria! I follow the signs. I know I'm getting close because I can smell the food. Voila! I look around to see tables and benches for where hospital visitors are concentration on eating their breakfast. I also see a buffet style table to my left and a juice bar straight ahead. I follow the buffet table with my eyes, trying to figure out where to start. I begin to my far left and walk over. I have a choice between plates and trays or Styrofoam carry outs. I choose carry outs, just in case I drop something. I pick up two. Then I grab a fork, knife, napkin, salt, and pepper all wrapped up in plastic and put them in my purse. I hear chatter in the background as I gather food for our breakfast.

I get Ben everything that's hot. I get myself two pancakes, some scrambled eggs, and two pieces of bacon.

Drinks.

I didn't ask Ben what he wanted to drink.

I decide to grab two cartons of milk.

I put the food down next to the register, so the cashier can see what I have and she starts pushing buttons on the register.

I notice a woman sobbing next to the cafeteria door.

"I can't believe someone did this to my baby. I'm going to sue whoever did this. I can't believe it. He broke his nose and broke his arm in half."

I straighten my back and make my eyes go wide.

I know who this is.

I pay for the food and walk over to the sobbing lady.

"Ma'am," I say.

She stops sobbing and looks at me. "Yes?"

"It was me who did that to your son."

She laughs. "But you are just a little girl. Now go and let me mourn." I stay put and say, "It's true. It was me."

I sigh and put the food down on the nearest table. I tell the same story I told the officer.

As I do, the lady puts her hand on her heart and her mouth is wide open.

After I tell my story, she says, "I'm so sorry my son did that to you. I hope he hasn't hurt or bothered you before."

I sigh and look down at the floor.

She obviously can read me because she says, "He has. When?"

I tell her about county fair.

I can see her disappointment. "That's the reason why he snuck out that night. He was grounded, too. Naughty boy."

She turns to looks at the person she is talking to. She realizes something because her eyes open wide and she looks back at me with a pointed finger.

"You are that girl that Landon met up in the Tetons." I sigh. "Yes. That's me."

She continues, "You went out with him once. He couldn't stop talking about you after that."

I look at the food and realize it's probably getting cold.

"I better get this up to my boyfriend."

I pick up the food and start walking out the door.

A hand on my shoulder stops me. "I'm glad you talked to me. Thank you."

I shoot a smile her way over my shoulder. I head out the door and find my way back to the elevators. I push the 3 with my elbow since my hands are full.

I make it back to Ben's room, open the door with my elbow, and shuffle around the door. "I'm sorry I'm late. I ran into…"

I look up and see the doctor standing at the foot of Ben's bed. I almost dropped a carry out at the sight.

"I'm so sorry. I didn't mean to interrupt."

"It's okay," the doctor said. "I'm done here. You need help?"

He takes the carry out that is about to drop out of my hands and also grabs a carton of milk. He places them on Ben's rolling table. I walk across the room and I see Ben watching me and smiling. I place the food I have in my hands on a table under the window sill. Outside, the sun is shining bright. The birds are flying in the sky, people are walking on the sidewalk, and cars are moving here and there, toward their destinations.

"I heard you were the hero last night," the doctor says.

I turn around and say, "Not really. I was just defending myself." "That's not how Ben sees it."

I blush and say, "Well, that depends on a point of view I guess."

The doctor looks at Ben and points his pen at me. "Humble, this one."

As the doctor picks up his clipboard and checks his patient list, he says, "Now, I have to go see the other guy that you broke."

He looks at me.

Ben stifles a laugh.

The doctor continues, "I feel bad for him. He has to go to jail after this place."

The doctor smiles and starts heading out the door. As he does, he tells Ben, "I'll have the nurse take that I.V. out as soon as possible and get you your pain meds."

The doctor is gone.

Ben is still looking at the door, and he says, "I like that doctor. He's funny."

I look in the carry out that the doctor placed on his rolling table. I have to make sure this is Ben's food. Sure enough, it is, and I roll the table over to Ben. I position it over his lap and bed. Ben pushes the button on his bed so he can sit up straighter to eat.

He looks at his food, then asks, "Fork?"

"Oh, yeah."

I take out the wrapped utensils from my purse and hand one to Ben. He uses the fork to stab the plastic to open it.

He starts eating.

He was hungry.

I do the same to get my fork out of the plastic and start eating my breakfast. As I'm eating, I wonder what the doctor told Ben while I was gone.

"What did the doctor have to say?"

Ben, with his mouthful, he says, "Oh, yeah."

He swallows.

"He said I can go home today. He's going to run the discharge papers and the prescription for my headache, give them to the nurse for me to sign, then I can get out."

"That's excellent news," I say.

Ben continues eating until it's all gone. Then he chugs his milk and sighs.

"That was good. I needed that."

I smile and continue eating my food. After I'm done, I toss the carry outs and cartons in the trash and move the table out of Ben's way. Within minutes, the nurse walks back in and takes the I.V. out of Ben's arm. I don't watch because I don't do well with blood or needles going in and out of the skin. I would not be a good nurse.

After she's done, Ben moves his arm. "Ahh. That feels a lot better."

The nurse smiles and says, "You could probably get your clothes on too. The doctor is printing out your discharge papers now."

She hands Ben his pills and a cup of water. He takes the pills and gulps them down with water. The nurse puts his cup on his table and leaves. He smiles at her and watches her leave. Then he looks at me.

I smile at him, pausing to check out his face, including the bandage on his nose.

"I would like to get my clothes on," Ben says.

I jump up, realizing what he meant. I grab the box of clothes sitting behind me. He gets out of bed and walks into the bathroom. I follow him with the box and sit it on the floor. I leave the bathroom and close the door behind me. I go back to the window to look outside and rest my head on the window. Sure is a nice day. Too bad Ben is in the hospital. Then it hits me hard that it's all my fault.

Sigh

Now... I wonder, am I really worth being his girlfriend? At least I know Landon is going to sit in jail, and he won't bother me anymore. I don't think Bill and Cole will ever be a problem again. They just got roped into Landon's evil plan, whatever his plan was to do to me. I'm glad I never got the chance to find out.

Ben opens the door with a swoosh, which scares me.

"Sorry. Didn't mean to scare you," he says as he lays the box and gown on the bed.

I put my hand on my heart, trying to calm it down.

"It's okay. I was just thinking about last night."

Ben walks over, puts his arms around me, and says, "It's all over. He's going to jail for what he's done. Crazy kook. You won't have to see him again."

I squeeze him and say, "I know. You're my hero. Thank you so much for saving me." Ben laughs, looks at me, and says, "Thank you for saving me. I thought you were a goner. All I could think about, as I lay there with my eyes watering was you and wondering what he was going to do to you."

Ben hugs me again. "I thought I was going to loose you."

I inhale his scent.

I laugh. "It made me so mad he hit you, so I hit him back. I wanted to make sure I hit him in the face too."

Ben laughs. "I'm glad you did." Then he kisses me on the head.

Chapter 31

$\mathcal{B}$en signed his discharge papers and got his prescription from the nurse. I call a taxi so we can have a ride back to the high school to pick up his car. Ben then drives me back to the dorm so I can change my clothes and pack up my stuff.

As I'm packing, Sarah and Jamie walk in. "We saw Ben downstairs. He told us everything. Are you okay?"

Sarah hugs me.

"I'm fine. I may be emotionally scarred, but I'm okay." I continue packing knowing that Ben is waiting on me.

"So you were being followed. I guess I need to be careful with what kind of guys I date," Sarah says.

I turn around and quickly say, "Yes! It's very important."

I look at Sarah and Jamie. "You need to be very picky on who you choose to date. Make a list of what you look for in a guy. That helps. Otherwise …" I turn back and finish shoving clothes in the garbage bag my mom gave me. "You'll end up like me. Don't be like me. Make the right choices now."

Sarah walks up behind me and puts her hands on my shoulders. "You made mistakes. We all make mistakes. It's just a matter of whether we learn from them or not."

I smile and put my hand on one of her hands.

Then I say, "I just don't wish this for any girl."

I start crying. All the emotions I had last night and this morning are pouring out of me.

Jamie and Sarah sit me down on the bed and hug me. I let it all out.

Other girls come in the room and see me.

"Jess!" they all exclaim.

I stop crying and rub my eyes. Each girl takes a turn and gives me a hug.

They all say, "I'm so glad you're not hurt. Are you okay?"

Word gets around fast. I'm sure by now the entire fair grounds will know about Ben and me.

On the way home, I call my parents. I might as well tell them what happened last night. They are just grateful that nothing seriously bad happened. I also convince them to let Ben stay the night with us since he lives by himself. I just want to keep an extra eye on him for the first night. My mom agrees.

Before we head back to my place, we stop at Ben's so he can pick up some church clothes and also work clothes, just in case Dad wants some minor help in the garage.

When we get back, my parents are outside, ready to give Ben and me a hug. It was nice to finally be home. My dad grills us some steaks and my mom makes her potatoes and green beans. I felt like I ate like a queen that night compared to the food I've been eating.

That night, both Ben and I take turns taking a shower, then we settle down for the night.

Ben and I cuddle as we watch a movie with the rest of the family.

After the movie, I show Ben the guest room and ask if there is anything else he needs like an extra blanket or a different pillow.

He smiles at me and gives me a hug. "Everything is just great. I'll see you in the morning."

We kiss. The last time I got a kiss like this was when I burnt my hand at Ben's house. My limbs feel weak.

"I'll see you in the morning," Ben says.

I'm still standing at the doorway, trying to get the feeling back in my knees.

"Yeah. I'll just head to bed."

I'm still standing in the doorway. Why won't my legs move?

Ben laughs. "Need another kiss?"

I say, "Um, maybe. I can't move my legs from the first kiss, so maybe not."

Ben walks back up and kisses me again. This time harder and with more passion. I feel like melting to the floor now. Instead, I come back. I'm kissing him passionately and hard.

Ben groans then says, "We need to stop."

I stop kissing him and blush. "Sorry."

Ben laughs then hugs me.

I inhale his scent again and sigh. Something to help me fall asleep faster. I let go of him and head to bed. I lay in bed lingering with his scent and fall asleep.

When we go to church the next morning, everyone is asking about Ben's poor nose. He and I take turns telling the story. Everyone says that they are glad we are safe and sound now.

We grab our usual pizza afterward and head home. This time, as we approach our house, I see two more cars parked in the driveway.

"Who's here?" I ask my mom.

"I don't know. Why don't you ask Ben?" she says.

I look at Ben surprised.

"Surprise again!" he says.

"What's going on?" I ask.

"You'll see," Ben says as he helps me out of the car.

He leads me into the house, and I hear, "Surprise!"

I see Liv, Jack and Dave in the kitchen all looking and smiling at me.

"What's this?" I ask.

Dave puts his arm around me. "It's a surprise going away party for you. Your mom got the pizza, and we brought everything else!"

I smile.

I see chips, pop, assorted fruit, and a banner hanging on the wall that says "Good Luck!" Since Dave has his arm still around me, I hug him first. Dave hugs me back. I'm in his hug longer than what I want to be, but Ben says, "Uh, Dave. That's enough. Let her go."

He lets me go and says sorry to Ben. I hug Jack and Liv next, and last but not least, I hug Ben.

I whisper, "Thank you. Thank you for this."

Ben lets go of me and says, "I planned this before..." He puts his hand on his nose, and then says, "I'm glad it still worked out though."

I hug him again.

We partied and enjoyed the time together the rest of the afternoon. I was sad when it was time for everyone to go.

"We hope to see you around your winter break," Jack and Liv say.

Dave says, "I hope to see her sooner than that. I like it when you are around. I've never seen Ben so happy. Even with that broken bump on his face."

I look and smile at Ben.

Ben blushes and says, "Why do you have to embarrass me like that, Dave?" Dave answers, "Because I'm your best friend. That's what best friends do." I laugh.

Dave gives me a hug again. This time it's reasonable.

"Good luck, shorty," he says as he walks down the steps to his vehicle.

I turn back to Ben. I start crying. I don't want him to go yet.

I hug him.

Ben says, "I'll see you on Saturday. I plan to help you unpack into your dorm. I'm not officially saying good-bye to you yet."

I cry, "I know, but I already miss you."

Ben squeezes me tight, then lets go and kisses my forehead. "I'll call you when I can," he whispers.

He walks down the steps to his car and gets in. I'm on the deck crying as I watch him drive away.

The rest of the week was long and painful for me. I pack up almost my entire room. I know it's hard on my mom, as well, because she's been making me my favorite dishes all week. I thought I was ready to go to college, but now that it's time for me to go, I don't feel ready. I want to stay home. I don't let my family see it. I stay strong and brave.

By Saturday morning, I have my car completely packed. There is no place for anyone to sit. Even my passenger seat is piled high to the ceiling. Ben comes in the morning and helps load last minute stuff into his car. Now it's time for me to say good-bye to my family. I know college is only two hours away, but I won't get to see them every night like I do now. I take my time and tightly hug each one good-bye.

Ben watches.

Tears are streaming down my mom's face. I am crying also.

Before I get in the car, I look back at my family and smile. They are standing in front of the house, watching me. It's like I'm looking at a real-life photograph. A "photo" I want to keep for the rest of my life. I don't want to forget.

I slide in the car with tears on my face and drive away. Ben is right behind me. He follows me all the way to the place I will call home for the next 4 years.

Once I get there, I can feel my excitement. I get my key and head to my dorm room. As I unlock the door and step in, I see two beds with two tiny closets, a sink, and two desks. On the opposite side of the room is a window. I go across the room and look outside. I see the campus police house across the way. That makes me feel safe. I turn around and see Ben with some of my stuff.

I sigh and say, "Let's just bring it all in then decide where they should go, so just put it on the floor for now."

While Ben and I unpack my car, Kendra shows up with her parents. It's now time for me to explain that Ben and I are dating.

I was right. It wasn't the Ben Kendra was expecting but she is still happy for me.

I let her take the bed closest to the window, and I take the bed closest to the door. We all manage to get everything unpacked and put away by lunch. Kendra, her parents, Ben and I all go out to eat at the Chinese restaurant down the road. When we get back, it's time for orientation.

Kendra says good-bye to her parents and Ben stays in our dorm. His job is to hook up my computer while we go to the orientation. It's a big clunky, old computer that my mom gave me. Ben says someday, he'll get me a more reliable and space-saver computer. For now, this will have to work, so Ben hooks it up.

Our orientation, which is at the basketball court, is a typical welcome and mainly focused on rules of the place. It only lasts an hour.

Kendra and I walk back to our room, and when we walk in, we see Ben playing solitaire on the computer.

"Looks like you got it to work," I say.

Kendra rubs his head and says, "Nice job, Ben."

Ben says, "You may have to talk to the college computer geeks for your firewall, but otherwise it's operable, the Internet works, and the printer is hooked up. You're ready to write papers."

Kendra and I look at each other with disgusted faces. The reality of college is setting in. Ben looks at his phone for the time. Does he really have to go?

He looks at me and sighs. "I would stay the night, but I have stuff to do at home before work and…" he points at his nose. "I have to see the doctor on Monday."

I look at him with sadness, hoping I can change his mind about leaving. Then I say, "Let me know how that goes."

I'm trying to be brave. Ben knows I'm trying to hold back tears, and he gets up from his chair and hugs me.

He whispers in my ear, "You'll have fun. I promise. College is supposed to be the fun part of life."

I'm crying now. "I'll miss you though."

"Aww," Kendra says.

I stop crying and wipe away the tears. I forgot she was in here.

Ben takes my hand and leads me out the door. We walk down the hallway to the main door, then step outside. In an instant, he twirls back around and hugs me again. And he see me crying.

"Please, stay."

Ben sighs. "I can't. My summer ends too. I have to work tomorrow." I didn't know that.

I sigh. "I understand."

He kisses my head and let's go of me. I wasn't quite done hugging him. I didn't get to inhale his scent.

"Wait!" I yell at him.

Ben stops and turns back around. I run to him and wrap my arms around his chest. He catches his step as I do and wraps his arms around me.

I hear Ben sniffle. "I'll come up and see you on my days off," he says.

In between my sobs, I say, "I'll come home on the weekends when you're off." "We'll keep in touch," Ben says. He loosens his hug and asks, "Walk me to my car." I nod my head.

We walk to his car with our arms around each other. I give him a hug and inhale his scent one last time. Ben does the same.

"I love you," I say.

"I love you, too."

We have one last kiss before he gets into his car. I am crying as I watch him drive away.

Synopsis: Jessica Brown is learning a new life and new love, but will her past leave her alone? Ben is looking for the right love. Is Jess the one? As the two get to know each other more over the summer, trouble brews in the background.

Author Biography: Jesse Apland lives in the windy city Casper, Wyoming with her husband and two little kids. Right now, she is currently a stay-at-home-mommy, but plans on working with the school district once her kids are in school. She stays busy with the kids, writing, and being involved with her church. She loves being outdoors, whenever her kids and the weather allow her to, doing whatever to stay active. Jesse also loves music whether it's singing or playing the piano.